JASPIERRE'S LAST CHANCE

Mixi J Applebottom

Printed in the United States of America

First Printing, 2016

ISBN 978-0-692-66640-1

www.MixiJApplebottom.com

Let's do it.
Let's be wonderful.

JASPIERRE'S LAST CHANCE

Chapter

One

Lucille was gone. Jaspierre stood up, leaning forward and placing her palms on the smooth, cold prison cell floor. Her father, Pierre, was dead. Very slowly, she started to do push-ups. Chance was alive.

It seemed completely ridiculous that she was in this cell. Yes, she had done her fair share of murdering, but her baby had been snatched from her before it had even suckled its first teat! She rolled over on the floor and began to do sit-ups.

Pierre had been murdered right before her eyes. She stood and started punching the large, heavy bag. Everything about meeting her father had gone terribly. He had looked haunted and terrified. She never got to prove to him that she was better than Mother. And he had been slaughtered, so she'd never prove it to him now.

Mere seconds had gone by before her entire life was destroyed. Pierre murdered, and her, bursting with baby, his body not even cold. Sirens wailed before the baby ever did, and she was caught.

Lucille was stolen, and Jaspierre tossed into prison. It was ridiculous. She started doing jumping jacks. The world appeared to have changed in the most vicious, unrelentingly difficult way. Yes, she had made some mistakes. She murdered, but even though he deserved it, it was still technically illegal. Couldn't they cut her some slack because Lucille was stolen? Because Pierre was murdered? But no, somehow, that was not quite how it worked. They should have just given her a ticket or a slap on the wrist. It was her first offense! Shouldn't everyone get to kill at least one person before they had to go to prison? She understood men like Chance needed to be locked up. But a successful woman like her? It made no sense. Everyone was a little naughty; what was next? Every single person who was speeding while driving locked up? Anyone who smoked in a non-smoking zone thrown into prison for years? *Where would they draw the line?*

Jaspierre would be locked up for the next six years. That was what the court decided was "fair." Edward, the same cop that had caught her baby bursting from between her thighs, did his best to find Lucille, but he just didn't have any luck. It was probably why he visited her so frequently. Jaspierre didn't bother hating Edward. He did the best he could. Besides, Chance was the freak who messed this all up.

And now Chance had Lucille. The most vicious, evil man on the face of the planet. Jaspierre was absolutely sure that he had destroyed that little girl. Could Chance handle a crying baby? There was not a single doubt in her mind that he could not. *Lucille was dead.* Smothered or shot or drowned. Probably during that first long night of crying, or when the very first fever set in, Chance would twist her neck until she popped. Jaspierre twisted with grief, counting to ten slowly, trying to contain it. The only thing she had wanted was a true family. She wanted her father, her baby, her kitties; and Chance had ruined it completely. It would never get better. The first year in this prison cell, she completely collapsed. It was quite a mental breakdown. Mother would never have understood it. Jaspierre sat, she sobbed, and didn't do a single damn useful thing. Could she have been more of an embarrassment? She was a shell of her former self, an empty broken woman. It took her body a full year to heal from the violent trauma of birthing a baby, and for her heart to harden itself.

The only thing she did during that time was pump milk every single day in the hopes that she would soon have a baby to feed. But one morning, when she was sitting sobbing and pumping milk for a baby that was stolen away, she realized she had no more milk to give. And how useless was it? Little Lucille might not even be drinking from a bottle anymore. She would be on solid food. She could be walking, talking; she wouldn't be an infant any longer. Except surely Lucille was dead. *She was dead.* Jaspierre finally accepted it. And that was the moment when Jaspierre remembered that she could be doing more. More than *nothing*, more than *milking herself*, she could be getting ready. That was the first day she started pushups. That first week, she could barely do ten at a time.

When she first went to prison, her belly, recently emptied from baby, was still quite large. When she sat and did nothing for an entire year, her body suffered. But now that it had been through two years of this daily regimen, her stomach had grown firm and thin. Her arms had grown large and strong. Her will, once broken, had returned with a vengeance. In fact, it was when she finally started caring again that she was able to remember that prison for the very rich could be quite different from prison for the average person. Spend a few dimes and it could be quite similar to one of those fancy clubs. Many of the prisoners played tennis and drank wine at the poolside. More like rehabilitation at a spa than prison. It amused Jaspierre to no end that she spent the first year rotting in a regular prison cell. Where had her mind gone to that she would allow herself to languish in such a way? It cost her an astounding ten thousand or more each month to be in the fancy prison. But the food was decent and she had a private room and was allowed to use the gym. She only went at night, refusing to speak with other guests, ahem, prisoners.

And her behavior had been good. So they said that instead of three long, endless years left of her sentence, she only had one left. While she was in that plain cell the very first year, she found herself thinking about Lucas. He had taken captivity so incredibly well. She had never considered this before, having never herself been locked up for years at a time. But now, now she knew. Her biggest regret was not letting him out earlier. He didn't really deserve this kind of punishment. But it was too late; she couldn't apologize to Lucille's father because he was dead. Chance was a virus that would catch and kill everyone she loved. But now she was at her peak. *So bring it on.* He consumed most of her plans. She would take him home and kill him slowly, patiently. His punishment would be no shorter than hers; the loss of everyone he loved and four years imprisonment at the very least. In her imagination, she had skinned, mutilated, and gutted him thousands of times already.

Jaspierre was preparing--preparing to get her daughter back, even though she'd just be a corpse. Getting back Lucille meant she had to face Chance. And so, she got ready. She went back to push-ups, this time one-handed. Her lean body had grown hard with muscles. Jaspierre never had been fit like this in her entire life.

One more year until freedom. And one more year until she slaughtered Chance.

CHAPTER

TWO

Edward stood in front of the two large metal doors, waiting with two cups of coffee in his hand. He had been waiting for this day for a very long time. In his mind, a grievous tragedy was about to be righted. Jaspierre stepped out of the large metal door, and it was the first time he saw her in regular clothes in the last four years. She was wearing a loose red dress and tall black heels. She had on no wig, instead embracing her long grey and brown hair. She looked amazing; the muscular definition of her arms, legs, and her excellent ass took his breath away for a moment.

"Hi, Jaspierre," he said, trying to play it cool.

"You can give me a ride?" she said. "I could go for a ride." She had the cutest little smirk, and her eyes lingered on him for a moment.

His heart pounded. "It seems like prison did you pretty good; you look fantastic."

"This dress is like five sizes too big now. Well, consider me rehabilitated."

"You ready to go home?" he said.

"No. I'm going to go to work." She really didn't want to go home. As far as she was aware, Dru was still in her house; perhaps the home was littered with ruppies, and, quite frankly, she didn't want to deal with him. Not yet, at least. She had not been able to get in touch with him for the last six months, and that concerned her greatly. She was certainly not going to take Edward to her house. Dru had been running everything while she was in prison, visiting regularly, but somehow, in the last few months, she could feel something had changed. It was extremely likely that any confrontation with Dru could end in bloodshed. Edward didn't need to see that at all. He, being an excellent, moral man, would handcuff her and drag her right back to her cell.

So instead, he dropped her off at Kyller and Co. It was foreign to her after all this time to walk up the marble steps, through the glass doors. In fact, she couldn't recognize the place. Everything had been redone; floors, walls, even the secretary had been changed.

"Hello, I'm Jaspierre," she said, standing her

JASPIERRE'S LAST CHANCE

tallest and attempting to look at her most
powerful.

"Do you have an appointment?" the
secretary said with a forced smile.

"I, I am the owner. I am Kyller, I'm *the
Kyller* in Kyller and Co." Jaspierre clicked her heels
crisply on the floor. "Do you understand what I
mean? Has my office been redone also?"

"I... I... I... I," the secretary said, extremely
nervous. "I'll buzz the CEO and let him know you
are here."

"Who is the CEO?" Jaspierre asked, a bit
startled. CEO was *her* job. She was, as far as she
still knew, the owner of that title. Surely they
would have had to notify her if they removed her
position? "Actually, instead of buzzing me up, I'll
stop by the office." She turned and walked up to
the elevator, stepping inside and pressing the
button for the top floor. The secretary mumbled
some sort of complaint, but Jaspierre didn't
particularly care what she thought. How could
there be a new CEO?

The elevator purred underneath her feet.
She considered what this meant. Had she been
fired? Surely they would have had to contact her.
Yes, she had been in prison, but she had still been
running her office. Or at least she *thought* she was.
Her secretary met with her every Friday and they

would discuss business and sign papers. *Where was he?*

By the time she got to the top, and the doors slid open, a security officer stood in front of the office. There was a new blond secretary sitting at a desk. Where was *her* secretary? The man who had come to prison with papers and discussed strategies with her? Where was *he?* The office door was lined with gold letters on the glass. Jaspierre gasped as she recognized the name instantly. Dru Valentine Brummel. *Fuck.*

Dru had her motherfucking job. Maybe she *should* have gone home first. Her mind whirred. If everything her secretary told her was a lie, then she was fucked. The security officer ushered her back into the elevator, and they slowly sank back to the bottom floor. Jaspierre didn't bother saying anything at all. What other lies had been told to her? *What the hell had happened?*

CHAPTER

THREE

Jaspierre called a cab. She had intended that her secretary would run and grab one of her many vehicles. One thing was obvious: he had been lying to her for quite some time. How long? Was it years? Was it months? *Fuck*. How much worse could it get? She stood outside Kyller and Co., her mother's company, her company, her family's legacy. And she waited for the yellow cab to draw up. Was her legacy lost forever? She stepped into the cab and sat down. Her fingertips pressed into her temples as she tried not to panic. It was about an hour drive, and very slowly, they made their way down the dirt road. Finally, she recognized the rock wall that curled around her mansion. When they drove up to the gate, it did not automatically open for her. She got out and put in her code; it wasn't a surprise to her that it didn't work. However, she remembered the overrides.

So, finally, the gate slid open, but it squeaked and rattled. Why the hell hadn't it been maintained? Blood was rushing to her ears. *How bad was this going to be?* She climbed back in the cab and rode up the long driveway. When she had been put in prison, the road was smooth, perfect in every way. Now it was riddled with salt marks, potholes, and cracks. She could feel her heart start to pound. *Stay calm. Stay very calm. Now is not the time to let your rage fly free. Wait for the perfect moment.*

The serval bushes that normally grew perfectly in front of the long marble steps up to the ornate carved door had been chopped down. Jaspierre clenched her fist and counted to ten, slowly trying to calm herself. It would take five years to grow those bushes back to that state. *Five years.* It was a new form of prison, waiting for her bushes to grow. Dru had declared war. How long ago did he do this? At what point had he begun to hate her?

She got out of the cab and walked up the marble steps. Her hand froze as she touched the handle of the door. If the bushes had been cut down, and her secretary had lied about her job, then where were Tessa and Ikali? *Fuck.* It seemed very unlikely that they were inside. The hairs on the back of her neck rose furiously. The door was left unlocked. Her throat grew dry and she suddenly lost the urge to call them. Tessa and Ikali were certainly gone. She stepped inside and looked around. Her previously polished marble floors were scuffed and dirty. She turned and went up the stairs to the right and peered in her room. It had been destroyed. Her massive bed with the four wooden posts each a servals in various positions. The one licking its paw had its face burned. The sitting serval was crushed. The third one stood on its hind legs, its paws lifted as if ready to bat at an invisible fly; well, it used to. Now it was splintered as if hacked at by an ax. The final cat with bared teeth had been coated in red paint. The bed had been snapped, the mattress sunken into the middle. She turned and looked down the hall. She didn't even want to look in her closet. *If she had only known this was going on!* She could have stopped him. But she didn't know; she never knew. She had been spoon fed lie after lie after lie. She never once suspected that her house was being reduced to ruins.

She stepped into her closet. The clothes and shoes were missing; only a few pieces left. She rummaged through her jewelry box and found only one remaining piece. A small golden chain

with a heart charm. The heart had the words
"*Mine Forever*" stamped into it. At the prison, they
had given her back the one piece of jewelry she
had on when she was arrested. Her father's ring.
And now she put on the second piece of jewelry
she still owned, Chance's declaration.

Mother's room had two large double doors;
one was swinging open freely. She looked inside.
It was dirty but not destroyed. Surely all of her
jewelry had been stolen, sold, or given away. She
didn't step into the room because two naked
women lay sleeping on Mother's bed. She turned
and walked back down the hall, glancing to the
right into her large exercise room. All of the
equipment had been removed, and a disco ball
was now installed in the ceiling, with two stripper
poles installed in front of the mirror. It figured
that once she was fit and ready to use the gym
equipment it would have been removed.

She walked back to the pool. The cargo net
and the jumping rock were gone. The pool now
looked plain and boring, still curling under the
pane of glass to the outside area. The pool was
also tinged with algae. *What to do next?* Dru would
be murdered, of course. But should she wait here?
Did he even know she was out of prison yet?
Hopefully, that secretary had forgotten about her,
just assuming she was a weirdo who wanted to

see the CEO. She walked to the large table that spiraled like a snake with little wooden planks. Thankfully, the table did not look destroyed. She wasn't sure that it was replaceable. The entire table was made out of wood, wooden gears, and wooden carvings. At the press of a switch, the conveyor belt would slide into the kitchen and slide out with food. The last time she used it was with Lucas.

Had Dru found the maze and the prison in the basement? Probably. She walked through the kitchen, which was a mess, and into her library. The books were strewn on the floor, half of them charred. Her desk was broken. But worse than that, the carved servals on both sides of the fireplace had been smashed. The cold, smooth marble had been destroyed for no reason. *No, they were destroyed for a reason.* The servals were all destroyed to send her a message. The message was received loud and clear: Jaspierre had been betrayed. The ear on the right serval was still intact, and the fireplace was open.

She walked down the concrete steps to the maze and the little prison. She could smell the stink of the room before she even reached the bottom. It smelled like sweat, shit, and urine. She stared into the maze; the white platforms and walls could move at her command if she so chose.

No longer white, they were smeared with dirt and blood and who knew what else. Inside the maze were people, at least Jaspierre thought they were people. They had been altered, taken apart, and put back together in a variety of ways. Those 3-D printers had been put to quite a bit of use. She wondered idly if he had finished Mother's work. But it looked like he had done his own variations. Outrageously long noses, tails, oversized ears. One lady had breasts that looked like long snakes. Would it have killed him to make a sheeple? All these people warped into creatures, and he refused to finish Mother's work. They were sneaking around the maze, avoiding each other. She wondered what they were doing in there. She turned and glanced at the three rooms on the right. In the first room, in Lucas's room, Arnold sat on the little cot. He looked the same as ever, thin and nervous. His room looked as tidy as he could get it. But also, it seemed that he had not been shown his bathroom.

In the room in the middle, a large Asian man was chained to the pairs of rings that went up the wall. He looked angry and wild. In the final room, a skinny redheaded girl sat. She had apparently gone under some sort of surgery and had her arms and back wrapped with bandages. Jaspierre wasn't exactly sure what to do with all of these people, so she left them. She had such a mess to deal with--the house, the people--and that didn't even include Dru.

She went back up the fireplace steps, carefully leaving the door exactly as it was. Then she walked out to the barn. The brick steps seemed about the same, nothing particularly special about them. The barn had no animals left in it. The ferrets, rabbits, mice, rats, and all the other feed for the servals were gone. The cages were gone, and in their place were several ways to detain people. A drugged man stood sleeping with his hands raised above his head, held by some sort of chain.

She walked past him quickly; she didn't want anyone to tell Dru that she had been here. She had to come up with a plan to deal with him. Peering at the operating theater, she saw both 3-D printers were whirring away. Printing up something, probably something to attach to that man. She stepped inside and peered at the pieces. They didn't look particularly special to her, nothing recognizable. The printer slowly spurted out tiny strings of DNA. Whatever it was looked... fleshy. She stepped back out of the theater and slid along the wall, pulling on the secret latch. Mother's office looked exactly the same. In fact, the only thing that had changed were more files and notebooks in another file cabinet. He apparently was taking notes and keeping records on all of the men and women that he was experimenting on. Dru was extremely like Mother in that way.

She walked to the garage that contained all of her vehicles, intending to take whichever one would be the most unlikely for anyone to notice missing. She'd hide out at a hotel room tonight and decide what to do. But her cars were gone, the garage was empty. Fifteen, maybe sixteen of them? That was a lot of cars to be missing. Fuck.

She supposed she'd have to get a cab again. She'd rather poke out her own eye with a fork. What the fuck had he done with her cars?

CHAPTER

FOUR

She decided to stay at a Motel Eight. Not really her normal style, but she it was a subtle place to hide. In the morning, she'd go speak with her banker so that she could buy another vehicle. How had Dru disposed of all of them? Sold them, likely. It was so irritating. Maybe she should report them all as stolen. Could she even remember what vehicles she owned? Their paperwork was in the safety deposit box, she thought. However, the key for that had been in her room.

It occurred to her that her key must have been stolen, and the title papers, and thus the cars. Perhaps they would even be considered a legal sale. What the hell was she supposed to do? And her guests. She couldn't burn twenty people in the fireplace. Besides, they weren't even dead. What a pain in the ass. She had no beef with these people; she didn't exactly desire to execute them. However, the giant investigation in her house would be a total nightmare, and to be sure, an investigation would follow. Elephant nose fellow would trumpet around that he had been mutilated at *her* house in *her* mansion. She'd never have a moment of peace again. *So what the hell were her choices?*

She asked for the largest room at the Motel Eight. She went up to whatever it was they called their penthouse suite. It had two king-size beds and a little kitchenette. And a hot tub, already full of water. *Gross.* But the room had plenty of space for push-ups and sit-ups. She was well into three hundred jumping jacks when it finally came to her. She could drug all those people and dump them somewhere. Of course, if Dru had been an idiot and let them know where her house was, then she'd still be fucked. There would still be an investigation. So maybe she'd have to interrogate them before she set them free. That seemed reasonable. Only execute the few that would hurt her or identify her. They'd just be people who experienced random acts of violence; they could work it out themselves. Well, one problem down, one left. What the fuck was she going to do with Dru?

JASPIERRE'S LAST CHANCE

Obviously, he needed to be punished. But how? How exactly was she going to destroy him? She really had to think it through. Maybe she should talk to Arnold before she let him go. *Oh yeah, maybe she couldn't let him go. He knew too much.* Of course, she never really had a beef with him. They'd have to talk it out. She sat on the floor and started on sit-ups. She wasn't exactly keen on killing. It was too much of a fucking pain in the ass to go to prison. Keeping people alive was useful for that reason alone. Perhaps prison had made her gun shy. She knew it was rare to murder and then land in the can. In fact, of all the people she had met, she was the only one who actually ended up doing time after killing someone. Plus she learned a lot, and frankly, that was a freak accident--a cop showing up the very moment she had shot a man. As anyone who speeds regularly knows: sometimes, a cop will issue a ticket.

She rolled over and decided to do another hundred-set of push-ups. It was so nice to be out. And look, she hadn't even been obsessing over Tessa or Ikali or Lucille. She had so many other problems. This might have made her sad, except she really needed a break from thinking about Lucille. She would find Lucille and Chance soon. Suddenly, she froze mid push-up.

Tessa and Ikali. What *had* happened to

them? How could she just brush off them missing? She collapsed to the ground and drew herself into a ball. Had she grown so cold that her closest companions no longer mattered to her? *No, it wasn't that.* She had been gone a long time. She couldn't spend another moment crying. Her home was ruined, Dru had destroyed her job, her family was gone. Tessa, Ikali, Pierre, Lucas, and Lucille. She didn't cry because if she got started, she would never ever stop. She counted to ten slowly and then started another round of sit-ups. It was time for her heart to grow cold. Vengeance would be hers.

In the morning, Jaspierre got a cab to go to the bank. What she found out horrified her more than anything else that happened. All she had left in her account was five hundred thousand dollars. *Five hundred fucking thousand dollars.* Where were her millions? Where were her billions? She was bankrupt. *Holy shit*, she couldn't even liquidate her assets--her cars had already been sold. Not that she would ever consider selling her house--but it turned out Dru had somehow managed to get a lien on her home. Was her company no longer profitable? She owned most of the shares; that alone should have been giving her ten million dollars or so every year. Her job as CEO paid out another twenty million or so. She didn't exactly pay attention to the pennies and dimes.

At this very moment, she really wished she had. She really wished she had paid attention to the pennies and the dimes that Dru had been pilfering from her very pocket. He had squandered all her money. It was extremely unlikely that he would be able to pay her back in any lifetime. Much less his *very* shortened lifetime. She tried to count to ten but couldn't focus. Five hundred thousand dollars would not even be enough to fix her home. She cringed at the idea of having to live in that wonderful house with her smashed servals, her destroyed bed, her cut-down bushes, and unpolished floors. *Were there any cars that cost under a hundred thousand?* She had to get her job back. And she had to make them pay.

It seemed that she would have to ambush the little monster. Her cell phone suddenly rang. She was so startled she practically fell over. She checked it, and it was Edward.

"Hi," she said in a dreary tone.

"Hey, I wanted to see how your first day out was going."

"Well, the house is a bit of a mess. So I've got some stuff to work out," she said.

"How is the office?"

"Things have changed around there a little.

But I think it'll all get smoothed out soon enough."

"Has Chance tried to contact you?" he asked nervously.

"Are you calling as a cop? Or are you calling as a friend?"

"Which one do you want me to call as?"

"I don't need a cop. Although I might be able to tolerate a friend. That said, no, Chance hasn't said hello. I almost wish he would."

"You know what? On the one hand, I wish he would so we could find Lucille. On the other hand, I am just so damn happy that you are not in danger," he said, relief flooding his voice.

"Yeah, at least I'm safe," she lied to him. She wouldn't be safe until Dru was locked up, and his experiments removed from her house, and Chance killed. But, whatever made him happy. "See ya around."

"Okay," he said. She hung up the phone and lay back on the cheap motel bed. She was out of prison but broke, and she needed to catch fucking Dru. She was going to punish that man.

Chapter

Five

Dru drove up to the mansion, to his mansion, in the sporty black Lexus. He hopped out and stepped inside the unlocked doors. He had had another successful day at work. That company tossed money at him like he was the king of the world. He had never been a wealthy man before, but it had grown on him quickly.

He shut the door behind him and shouted, "Hey, ladies, I'm back." They didn't reply; probably still drugged or asleep. He didn't really care. These were the best years of his life. He thought about what he was printing in the barn. He decided to try to make elephant ears to put on that man in the barn. If that worked out, he could add a nose and have a proper elephant man. He had been thinking about how exactly to attach them when he heard a little clattering rattle. Were the ladies awake? He walked up the large marble steps on the right past Jaspierre's room with a sneer. He walked all the way down to Severina's room.

"Ladies?" He peered in, but they weren't there. He turned, walking back down the long hallway, down the marble steps, and into the kitchen. He grabbed an apple and started munching. It wasn't a good one, so he set it on the counter and grabbed a different one. This one was green, so hopefully, it would have a little more flavor. He crunched into it. It was sweet and tart, an excellent apple. A long scraping rattle called him again. It sounded like metal scuttling against something. Which room was it coming from?

Could be the library or near the pool. He decided to walk down by the pool. Hopefully, the ladies were skinny-dipping. "Ladies?" He walked past the elaborate dining hall and towards the pool. He didn't see anything or anyone. Well, maybe they had gone downstairs to the prison. Seemed kind of an odd choice, but who was he to judge the ladies?

He wished he could recall their names, but other than remembering that they were slutty, he couldn't come up with any other details. The scrape paused for a moment and then rattled louder. It was definitely a metal-scraping-on-something sound near the kitchen. Honestly, it was kind of creeping him out. Not that he'd want to admit that. Hopefully, no one had gotten out of the basement. What if the ladies let out that big Asian man? That guy was pissed.

As he walked towards the kitchen, he saw Jaspierre. She was thin, muscular, and she was staring into his eyes in the most terrifying way. In her right hand, she held a long sword. The tip of the sword was rattling behind her on the marble floor. She didn't say anything; she just walked towards him, eyes locked on his, a frozen half-grin on her face. *When did she get out!?*

He turned and ran to the front door, grabbing it and trying to open it. *Fuck this shit.* He was getting the fuck out of here. But the door wouldn't open. It was locked. He had not locked it. It was one of the few doors that he could not figure out how to lock. *But Jaspierre knew how to lock it.* He turned and looked and she was steadily and calmly walking towards him, blade rattling behind her. He scrambled up the marble steps. What he needed was time to figure out a plan.

"Hi, Jaspierre. I wasn't expecting to see you." His feet were practically tripping over each other as he scrambled down the hall, frantically looking for an exit. "How was prison? I'm sorry I haven't visited in the last few months... it's been busy."

She didn't say anything. But her smile grew creepier and her sword seemed to rattle louder and more intensely. Dru kept envisioning the blade slipping into his stomach and his guts falling out of him onto the floor. Would he feel each coiled rope slip out from his belly? Or would the shocking pain of the blade be all he would feel?

"Jaspierre, let's be reasonable now. You were in prison! I'm sorry the house is a mess, but this is fixable. We can work this out." He threw open the double doors to Severina's room, to his room. Maybe he could jump out the window? The clattering rattle skipping across the marble floor came closer and closer.

He ducked into the closet. Maybe she wouldn't find him? *Holy shit, this idea was terribly stupid.* He racked his brains for another spot he could run to, but he couldn't think of anything. He glanced around the closet frantically. There had to be a hidden sword in here. Or perhaps some other way to defend himself. His gun! Had he put a gun in here? *Shit.*

No, he put it in the dresser, next to all of Severina's old sex toys. *Fuck.* Jaspierre already stood in Severina's room. She was walking steadily and intently towards the closet. He grabbed the box that was sitting next to him, threw it at her head, and tried to run past her.

She ducked easily and continued to follow at her slow, steady pace. Frantically, he let out a scream as he ran down the hall. He rattled the front door. *Fuck.* He ran towards the pool. He wasn't exactly sure what he was going to do at the pool. Maybe he could drown her? *Maybe couldn't.* His heart was racing. How would he even get her in the water? *Fuck.* What the hell was he supposed to do? That clacking scrape was catching up to him steadily. He struggled to make a decision. Finally, he decided to jump into the water himself. What was she going to do? Stab him while he swam? *Ha.*

He swam towards the glass wall. He wasn't a particularly strong swimmer, but he only needed to swim under the glass to the outside pool. And then he could run to the front, hop in the Lexus, and get the fuck out. He dove down, his hands grasping the glass, pulling his body under and through, and he popped out the other side. He couldn't see her anywhere. *Yes!* He made it; he had escaped. He grinned and shook himself dry. Glancing behind him, he saw nobody. *Like she could fucking catch him now!*

He walked briskly around to the front of

the house, and just as he was making the last corner, she stood in front of him, staring at him with her cold, dead eyes and the half-grin smile. His heart dropped to his stomach. "Jaspierre, I think we should talk. It's not what you think! It's not. This is all just a big misunderstanding." She smiled and lifted the blade, pressing it to his chest. He raised both hands in surrender but frantically looked side to side. Couldn't he just run? Which way? If he could just get around her, he could hop into that car.

She stood there, her grin growing. Sweat mixed with sour pool water dripped from his forehead. His clothes were wet and gushy. She backed off just a little, and he stepped around the corner of the house. She followed. He made a dash for the Lexus. He tugged on the handle, trying to rip open the door. But it was locked. The blade suddenly pressed against his back. He trembled but moved no further. She leaned in close, her lips pressed to his ear. "Aren't you going to welcome me home?" she whispered.

She pressed the blade tighter against his back and the tip slipped through his wet shirt and into his skin. He writhed in pain. It was like his soul had escaped his body. His scream echoed against the building. Death would be swift; as soon as she plunged that blade into him the second time, he wouldn't be around anymore. Her phone rang suddenly. Dru trembled. He was pinned to the car as she answered it.

"Hello?" she said. After a brief pause, she answered, "Well, not tonight, but I'll come over tomorrow." She laughed. A long pause. While she was listening to whoever she was talking to, he tried to adjust his position. Maybe he could turn fast and then punch her in the face. He wasn't much of a fighter, but desperate times... "Okay, it'll be fun. See you then." She adjusted the blade as she dropped her cell phone back into her pocket. Dru let out a howl of pain.

"This is just a misunderstanding, Jaspierre." He writhed with agony. Her face twisted with amused fury. She pulled something from her pocket and pressed a wet rag across Dru's face.

"We are going to have so much fucking fun." She said. He couldn't reply; his world was already going dark.

Jaspierre's Last Chance

CHAPTER

SIX

Jaspierre ran her fingers through her long hair. Once Dru was unconscious, she had to decide where to put him. Her maze and prison cells were full of people. She didn't particularly want to move any of them to the barn, and her three prison rooms had guests. She dragged him down the stairs anyway. Maybe she could move the redheaded girl to the maze.

She thumped his body carelessly down the stairs and then remembered. Arnold. Well, worst-case scenario, they could bunk together. Best-case scenario, Arnold would help her out. One button press later: "Hey, Arnold. Why did Dru lock you down there?"

"Hello?" He sounded utterly confused. "Who am I talking to?"

"It's Jaspierre. I got out of prison. I want to

know why you're locked up."

"Well, Dru and I had a bit of a misunderstanding," he said, hesitating.

"I hate that fucking word. Misunderstanding. That could mean anything. It could mean you tried to kill him, it could mean you passed him the pepper instead of the salt. So *fuck* that. What I need to know is, are you with me or against me?"

"With you," he answered very quickly. Clearly, he wanted out.

"Yeah, I bet. I bet you are," she said, clearly annoyed. Anxiously, she drummed her fingers on the console.

"Jaspierre, you hired me. I didn't like what happened with Basel. And you're right, I don't have any reason to be loyal to you. Except that I'm sure we have a common enemy. And that's enough for me," he said frantically, trying to convince her. She could see him clicking his fingers and mouthing onetwothreefour. Thumb to pinky, then ring finger, then middle finger, and pointer. Back and forth in an unrelenting rhythm.

"I'm going to kill you if you fuck up. I don't have time for any drama. One wrong move, and your head is no longer on your body. Otherwise, salary would be the same, that kind of deal," she said to him, offering a business arrangement.

"Okay." And the smooth white wall in front of him slid open, revealing a smooth white hallway. He slowly started up the spiral staircase, and a solid wall at the top slid open.

She pressed another button, and the hideously loud noise of spray and the scent of bleach filled the air. "I'm surprised that this still works. It doesn't seem like Dru managed to keep anything working besides that 3-D printer." Arnold anxiously stood just inside the doorway, looking at a crumpled Dru on the floor.

"Would you take our honored guest to his presidential suite?" she said. Arnold grinned and dragged Dru down the stairs, slamming and crashing his unconscious body on every step, clearly enjoying every loud thwack. He shoved him inside the room that was still dripping with bleach water. The razor-lined doorway snapped shut crisply.

Jaspierre sat at the control table, staring into the maze. "I think there are ten of them in the maze. Two with noses, three with tails, snake boobs, the blank one, two with shaped ears, and then whatever those last two are." It was surely a freak show. The last two were – stuck together. It looked like he made those snake boobs on each of them and then stitched them together. *Really weird.* Why would Dru even do that? Why did

Mother do what she did? *If I knew the answer, I'd practically know the meaning to life.*

* * * * * * * * * * * *

Mother fucking shit. Chance climbed into a large black truck. He turned the key and the car hummed to life. *Mother fucking shit.* How could he after all this time miss it? How the fuck could he have missed it?

He had been preoccupied with a couple of ladies, but even that shouldn't have been enough for him to miss the most important day in the last four years. Jaspierre had gotten out of prison. How the fuck had he missed it? She was going to think he didn't care anymore. *But he did care!* He cared a bunch; he really, *really* cared. In fact, he doubted there was another person in the world who cared about Jaspierre as much as he did. He had planned to pick her up from prison on the day of her release. Wasn't that what a loving fiancé would do? He wondered if they let her keep her engagement ring. Those kind of details were hard to find out. He bet he'd see it on her finger after she was out. If she didn't have it, he could always go harvest another one.

Finding out the day of her release shouldn't have been difficult! In fact, he had a couple of guys who were supposed to be on top of it. But apparently not. He couldn't possibly be more frustrated. Now he was going to have to make the long thirty-hour drive without any preparation. *Fuck.* She was going to be pissed as all hell.

How can you wait four years for something and then miss it? *What the fuck was wrong with him!* He whirred onto the highway, pressing the gas hard. Getting a ticket would suck balls, so he only went five miles over the speed limit, resisting the urge to go faster. He glanced in the rear-view mirror, examining his own face. The skin was knotted and snarled, outlined in white and black tattoos. He slipped on his shades and his wide brim hat and turned up the radio.

He had spent the last four years hiding in Canada. It wasn't exactly his perfect plan, but it worked well enough. There were plenty of small towns, so he could flit from one to another. He usually only stayed a couple of months before he moved on to find another lady. Canada was full of sluts; who knew? In fact, most women were extremely accommodating, despite the fact that they didn't usually survive their little affairs.

In one instance, a husband came home early. That was exciting; he had never had a man walk in on them before. It turned out to be a short-lived but very fulfilling experience. Four years, waiting for his honey. He hoped that those years had done her good. Her round ass and big bulging titties; damn, she was hot. She had to be what? Thirty-two now? So young enough to breed a few more times.

Dammit. He had all these plans: Fireworks, a little enthusiastic meeting, and he'd take her back to his place. He had considered multiple times visiting her in prison or sending her a couple of letters. But, in the end, he decided it was best to surprise her. Surely, surely she knew that he was going to be around. That he would wait for her. Why wouldn't he wait for her? She was his true love. His childhood sweetheart. She was the one thing that consumed his mind day and night, night and day.

And he was fucking late. She was going to think he didn't have it for her anymore. That she didn't cook his goose, raise his flag, or pop his cherry. She was going to think, after the four years, that he didn't give a shit. And that pissed him the fuck off. Because he gave a shit. He'd give her all his shit. *Fuck yeah, couple of days from now, she'd be sitting next to him inside the truck and they'd be fucking like bunnies.* They'd run around Canada-Bonnie and Clyde style. Only twenty-nine hours to go.

CHAPTER

SEVEN

Jaspierre pulled up to the little brown house. It had a white picket fence and a dark blue doorway. It didn't look particularly small, although compared to Jaspierre's mansion, it was but a shed. But, compared to her prison cell, it was extremely roomy. She wasn't exactly sure how to feel about this. Her knuckles rapped at the blue door and Edward opened it and stared at her. She was wearing a long grey T-shirt dress that hugged her curves quite nicely.

"Did you go shopping? I can't imagine anything in your closet would've still fit you. You are so thin now," he said.

"Yeah, I grabbed a few things. I still have to get some suits. This obviously wouldn't be suitable for the office." She grinned, toying with the small golden heart necklace dangling between her breasts. On it was imprinted the phrase "*Mine Forever.*" It was a reminder.

"Well, come on in," he said. She stepped inside the doorway into a terribly quaint house. A bright colorful quilt was draped over the sofa. The place was generally tidy, but not clinical. The kitchen had a few dishes sitting on the counter. A large black recliner, obviously the favorite seat in the house, was worn. At the kitchen table sat several boxes, a few files sitting in front of each chair. The table was extremely over-sized. It probably sat ten people.

"Do you work at your table a lot? It seems too big for this little house." She immediately regretted insulting his house. But he didn't seem to mind.

"Oh, I got one that size not for parties or anything, but because it's so nice to spread out my files on. Come take a look," he said. He seemed almost giddy that she was in his house. They pored over the files. Most of them were not that exciting for Jaspierre, although Edward was very excited to show her. He had connected many files and murders to Chance. Jaspierre was neither surprised nor interested; in fact, a small part of her wondered how it was even relevant. *He killed people. So what?* It was just hookers or whatever. It was not like he murdered a president. *How did it even help?* Dead people don't tell tales; some would say that was part of the point of murdering them.

"The thing is, as soon as you went to prison, Chance's trail went completely cold. I can't imagine that he stopped murdering people. In his history here, it shows that he virtually never stops murdering people. He doesn't take breaks, he doesn't have time off. He is a steady serial killer. One or two a month, *pop, pop,* just like that." He paused. "That's why, I think, there are two options. Option one: he is still murdering people. This means, for some reason, I can't find him. Maybe he moved out of the country, maybe he holed up somewhere small where he didn't get caught yet. There's a lot of options, where he's just out of reach, but still murdering people. So eventually, he will get caught.

"The other option--I'm not sure if you are ready to hear this, Jaspierre. He might... he could... already be dead." He cringed, watching desperately for her reaction. He scooted his hand closer, just about to grab hers.

But she didn't go crazy. Or shout or cry. She just smiled very slowly. "He is not so easily killed." And that was that. They would not discuss the idea that Chance was dead again. "What is holding up the investigation? If he is in another country, for instance, how do we find him?"

"Well, that becomes the problem. We don't have the right kind of case to make a worldwide affair. We can't get the world to pay attention, not as far as I'm aware. But there is a chance if we throw some money at this..."

At this, Jaspierre stomach turned. She used to be a very, very wealthy woman. Edward seemed to believe that Lucille was still alive, but Jaspierre knew better. A serial killer couldn't raise her daughter. It was an impossibility. He'd have snapped her little neck the first time she whined. The only reason to find Chance was to give Lucillejustice. She clenched her fist until her knuckles turned white.

He seemed to notice the strained look on her face. "If you don't have cash for that, we can try to do something else. I didn't mean to assume. It's just that I really want to find her for you."

"How much do you think we need?" she asked somberly, her heart flipping in her chest. How hard would it be to get her job back?

"Probably a couple million. If that's too much, then we can focus our investigation more precisely. Private investigators, that sort of thing. If we knew which country he went to, it would be a hell of a lot less expensive. Did he ever say anything to you about wanting to go to Paris? Or...

I don't know, did he want to go anywhere? Without a starting point, it gets much more expensive."

She closed her eyes, lost in thought. A million dollars or more. If she was working, she wouldn't even bat an eye. Just a few years ago, she could have written a check. But she didn't even have that kind of cash. "You know what? He never wanted to leave the USA. He's pretty damn die-hard American. So I think that either he's still here or is close. Like Canada or Mexico. Also, he fucking hates to fly. It's too hard with all that security crap going on. So my guess is that he only went where he could drive."

"Do you think he'd have a preference? Canada or Mexico?" he said, looking excited. He kept leaning in closer to her. She could feel his eyes burning into hers. It made her cheeks warm. Something about that look in his eye made her think of Lucas. He didn't try to kiss her, but she could feel his desire trembling in the room.

"Mexico is hot. Canada's cold. Canada seems to have a lot of hunting. Mexico seems more like he could get away with anything. I think I'd lean towards Canada, but only because we're closer." She didn't say what she was thinking, that he'd want to be as close as he could so he could come get her. She indeed hoped that he would come and say hello.

"All right then." Edward smiled, leaning back in his chair. "I am going to send some emails to several places in Canada and Mexico. We will see if they've had an uptick in murders in the last few years. Maybe this will get us somewhere." He nodded towards the kitchen. A soft expression waded over his eyes. "You hungry?"

The urge to run and the urge to tear his clothes off suddenly and unexpectedly combated in her head. Why did he look so delicious and soft? Indecision struggled within her, and she suddenly hugged him. His body was unexpectedly warm, and her skin trembled. His heart was pounding and his lips drew near to hers. "I have to go home. I still have a lot of work to do tonight. Sorry, I can't stay." And with that, she left him wanting.

* * * * * * * * * * * *

Edward found himself obsessing over the beautiful millionaire, or was it billionaire? The hardness in her eyes did not detract from the beautiful brokenness he'd seen. That first year that she was in prison, not only was she completely unhelpful in talking about Chance, but she was going crazy. She would sit across from him with a cup of coffee, and it was like watching a rose bush catch a disease and slowly wither.

Jaspierre's Last Chance

She'd clawed at her own skin and tore out her hair. He was personally responsible for her breakdown. She was jittery, although there were no drugs found in her system. She was almost unable to form a sentence. This difficult violent trauma that she suffered was because of Chance. He took that brand-new infant of hers, not even an hour old yet, and stole the baby Lucille.

Edward was a man with many regrets. But this particular regret of being unable to save that baby haunted him. Her tiny newborn cry would awaken him in a cold sweat. She cried to him in his nightmares. He couldn't imagine what Jaspierre heard in hers. It was ridiculous that she could even look at him. For months, he couldn't even look at himself. But he *could* look at her and stare into her gorgeous haunted eyes while she sipped coffee. He watched her body change before his eyes as she hardened and suddenly strengthened herself. Not just physically, but her eyes stopped being so lost and haunted and instead took on a determined glint. Her comeback impressed him.

But underneath it all, he worried that the broken woman lurked just a breath beneath the surface. What would Jaspierre do once Chance was in prison? How would she survive it? The one thing that kept her going could very well slip through her fingers. Or, even worse, get her killed.

And yet, here she was out of prison. And somehow, even with the most traumatic things happening to her that any woman had ever had, she had blossomed. Her body was firm and beautiful, and her spirit was unbroken and bright. *But dark.* She was dark, and hate dampened the gorgeous beauty that she held within her. Edward didn't expect her to just recover. But he also had not expected her to be so intent on revenge. She is a bold woman, strengthening her body and preparing for war.

It terrified him that she was going to meet up with that man again. He was convinced that she was holding out information on him. She intended to kill that man. Not just kill him, but torture and destroy him. Edward knew this, and even though he wanted to stop her, he also wanted her to succeed. Would she be able to recover once that violent man was put behind bars? Put to death? Would she ever be able to start over?

She'd probably make an excellent mother. She was determined, smart, and beautiful. She'd do anything for her children, even kill for them. It was ridiculous. But it was part of why he was so magnetically drawn to her. He had never seen a woman after a child was snatched both break and recover with such vehement power. Would she ever have the chance to bear a child again? Somehow, his heart flickered at the thought that perhaps she'd hold his seed. Wouldn't it be beautiful to have a safe, happy family after all this craziness?

Maybe he could ease her pain. And maybe, just maybe, she would allow herself to be loved. He couldn't imagine that anyone had ever shown love at this point in her life. It was probably why her baby being stolen affected her so much more strongly than other women in the same state. He couldn't deny it; he had fallen for her at some point. He wasn't sure if it was when she sat across from him; intense, scratching, and absolutely nuts for her baby. Or if it was when she showed up one day for the meeting, drenched in sweat. And when he asked her why she was so sweaty, she just simply said, "I'm training."

And she did. She trained harder than anyone he'd ever seen train. Just two weeks later, he could see her form changing before his very eyes. And this beautiful broken woman rose like a Phoenix. She grew strong, she dropped that haunted look in her eyes, and picked up a new one. A new fantastic look of determination. She stopped scratching.

She was amazing.

Jaspierre's Last Chance

Edward wasn't sure she was ready to be loved yet. So he tried not to push the issue. Instead, he focused on the things that would make her happy: Lucille and Chance. He had done numerous searches for Lucille, but he just hadn't had any luck yet. Chance *should* be easy to find with those scars tattooed all over his face and the long string of dead women behind him. But it had been four years and all of the leads had dried up. His phone buzzed as his email connected to the server. One of the towns in Canada said they had no statistical increase in murders. Two of the police stations in Mexico said they also had no increase in murders.

As he was reading this, his phone rang. "Hello, Officer Ed."

"Did you send the email? About the guy murdering hookers, with the tattoos?"

"Yes! I did. Do you have any news?"

"Well, I don't know if I have your guy. But I have had an increase in the murder of women. They aren't hookers, but they are mostly women. However, they are spread out over kind of a large area. Do you think this could fit your guy?"

"It's possible. Send me what you've got," Edward said. He couldn't help but grin. With any luck, he'd have good news for Jaspierre. And just maybe, she'd flash him that beautiful smile.

CHAPTER

EIGHT

Jaspierre drove back to her house in her black Lexus. She was pretty damn happy to have her car back. But she was missing all the other things that made her happy. Money, Tessa, Ikali, Lucille, Lucas. Even Pierre. Life pretty much sucked. But at least she could take out some of her frustrations on Dru. And he deserved every single fucking one of them.

When she walked into the house, she noticed immediately that the floors been swept. They had not yet been mopped or polished but swept. A grin creeped across her face. "Hey, Arnold, don't work yourself to death!"

Arnold popped his head in through the kitchen. "Hey, Jaspierre. I'm so glad to have you back. I've been cleaning the kitchen." He wore two pairs of rubber gloves, and his long, thin, grey hair had been put up in a scarf. He wore an apron and rubber boots. "What would you like for dinner?" It seemed, for the moment, his counting tic had taken a little break.

"A sandwich is fine. *Dammit*. We have a whole fucking group of people to feed. Have you fed any of them?" she said.

"I hadn't thought of feeding them. I'll get right on it," he said, but his eyes flickered back and forth. He clearly would prefer to keep cleaning.

"Look, we both want this place cleaned up. How about you work on that, and I'll make the food?" she said. Then she got to work making a pile of sandwiches. After making about twenty of them, she decided she absolutely did not want a sandwich for lunch. She threw in a frozen pizza and waited for that to cook.

Before she could work on Dru, she'd have to decide what she was doing with all these people. What exactly was her plan? She wasn't even sure. Her fingertip scraped on the broken marble serval as she clicked its ear. Fucking asshole had to destroy the carving. She carried the large tray of food down the stairs in the fireplace.

Feeding two of the prisoners was quite easy; she pressed the button and two dumbwaiters opened. She stuffed two sandwiches in each and a bottle of water, then pressed another button. In the room with the Asian man and the room with the red-haired girl, the two dumbwaiters opened. The red-haired girl, still coated in bandages, walked over, and using her bandaged hand, tried to lift the bottle and the sandwich out of the dumbwaiter. She had a lot of difficulty but managed to get them both out of the little box. Asian man could not reach, being chained to the rings on the wall. Jaspierre pressed a button, and a little red dot blinked on the wall in the room with the red-haired girl. "Okay, that red dot is a marker for how you can use the bathroom. If you hold your hand – well, your skin onto it for ten seconds or so, the bathroom door will open. Pay attention to where it is because I won't show it to you again." She pressed another button and the dot in Dru's room also blinked. She considered not telling him about his bathroom, but she was really sick of the nasty smell down here. "Dru, you pay attention to that red dot also."

She didn't bother telling the Asian man because he wasn't able to move much anyway, still chained tightly to the metal rings in the wall. She would deal with him soon enough. She looked at the large swarm of people in the maze. They were still avoiding each other. She stared at the one with the long snaky tits. "Okay, you with the long boob things, why are you guys avoiding each other? What are you doing in there?"

The girl looked up, very surprised. "We are supposed be playing a game? Survivor gets released?" She had a long annoying whine to her voice, and somehow, every sentence was a question.

"Okay, circus freaks. Listen up. Game over. I'm going to put a bunch of these sandwiches in the middle of the maze. Please watch your toes." She pressed a few buttons and slid the tray into another large white box. The wall slid shut, smooth as ever. The sandwiches made their way to the center of the room in the maze. The maze was about as big as two football fields, much bigger than the house up above. The maze slid under the driveway, providing support for the perfectly smooth paved path.

Or rather, the cracked, salted, and destroyed pavement. She wrinkled her nose when she remembered the state of her driveway. With a whirl of a few dials, the maze rearranged itself. Soon it was one open room with a few cubicle-sized areas blocked off by walls. "All right, so that'll have to do for bedrooms or whatever. Be nice to each other while I figure out what to do with you. Oh! Actually, please step under the tent." She made a larger shelter out of walls and platforms, pressed the button, and the entire room suddenly was sprayed down with water and bleach. Including their food. "*Fuck. Shit.* Sorry, guys. I forgot about the stupid sandwiches." There was a purring reply as many of them tried to talk at once to her, but she simply turned off their microphones.

Fuck. She had to decide if she was going to go make another batch, or just let them eat the soggy ones. Eh, she could bring more later. If they were hungry, they could pick at the waterlogged ones. The Asian man seemed an easy to spot to start. Would these people be up for release or execution? She wasn't particularly enthusiastic about either option, both seeming incredibly time consuming and annoying. She did not have time for all this shit. She had baby-killing Chance to hunt down.

"Hey, dude. Do you know where you are?" she spoke into her headset.

Big Asian opened his eyes, looking around. "Who is talking to me?"

"Do you know where you are?" Her voice was sharp and unfriendly.

"Who the fuck is talking to me?"

"Either you know where you are, or you don't," she said, beginning to get irritated.

"Who. The. Fuck. Are. You?" He paused at

each word, shouting angrily. She clicked the microphone off. She didn't really need to argue. She just needed to find out if they knew her name was Jaspierre, and they were in her house. The rest, she didn't give a shit about. Maybe she just hadn't talked to the right person. The red-haired girl didn't seem like she was able to leave yet. Her bandages were still blood-soaked. A few clicks of a button and a box slid open with new bandages for her. Jaspierre didn't bother questioning anyone else. Did she even really care that much? Perhaps she should just run a blade through them all and move on. Wasn't that the point? She was ready to move on. Besides, she had to kill Chance, and that was the only real priority.

So she walked upstairs and shut the fireplace the door carefully. It didn't appear to be broken and latched just fine. She reached up and clicked the serval's ear. The door swung open just like it was supposed to. Carefully, she shut it again. The fireplace, now that it was visible again, was full to the brim of skeletons. *Dick head.* Didn't he know you could only burn them one at a time? For a man as smart as Dru, he sure could be an idiot sometimes.

She walked through the kitchen and grabbed a slice of pizza. Thankfully, Arnold had taken it out of the oven or it probably would've been burned to a crisp. He had taken his half and was probably bleaching it before he ate it. She grinned. It was nice that he was obsessed with cleaning, but it sure was funny. She didn't bother to search for him because she suddenly remembered there were two naked women in her mother's room last time she went up there. Were those ladies still around? She walked down the hallway into the room. Well, it appeared they had left. Mother's room was the largest bedroom in the house, and Jaspierre let her eyes linger on the white bed. It hadn't been destroyed and she was happy. Mother's room was one of the few places she felt like Mother actually existed. Arnold hadn't cleaned in here yet.

There was that guy in the barn, though. She walked out to the barn, only after drawing a scarf around her face. No need to be easily recognized. She walked into the barn and the man was still there, arms raised above his head. But instead of being asleep, he was awake. "Do you know where you are?"

"Where am I?"

"Where do you think you are?" she said. He looked wild-eyed and rattled against his chain as if he was about to run. Jaspierre suddenly had pang of worry. When she was a child, she let Jasper out, and Jasper tried to kill her. When she was a child, she let Pierre out, and Pierre did not try to kill her. She let Basel out, and he tried to kill her and did kill her father. If indeed, two out of three people let out of cages would try to kill her, then this was a stupid game to play. She should just run a sword right through them, drop 'em in in the fireplace and, with a woof, they'd be gone.

"I don't know. The last thing I remember I was... I... I'm not sure. I think I was... Walking. Walking home? I guess. I guess that's what I was doing. Where am I? How did I get here? What are you going to do to me?" He was nervous. His eyes grew even more frantic, glancing left and right. He looked like a horse that was just about to kick.

"Has anything happened to you since you've been here? Do you know where you live?" she asked, considering her options.

"That doctor kept giving me shots. I don't really remember the rest. I'm awful hungry. Do you have any water?" He was straining against the chains, pulling them as hard as he could.

"Where do you live?" she said.

"I live in one of those cabins. Up that winding road. Do you know?" His eyes grew wide with frightened recognition and he started to shout, "I know who you are. I remember you! You helped that doctor. You told him to do this to me! I remember. *Jaspierre!*"

JASPIERRE'S LAST CHANCE

She stepped back suddenly. So this was part of Dru's plan. To make all of these victims think that she was the monster. That Jaspierre was the one ruining their lives. Probably his plan was to toss her back in prison as soon as she got out. *Well, well, well.* She pulled a knife from beneath her skirt and turned to look at the man. "I am so sorry. This is really quite unfortunate."

And she drove the knife into his neck, killing him.

Jaspierre's Last Chance

Chapter

Nine

Edward considered his options. He wasn't exactly supposed to date a felon on probation. In fact, he would be risking his career. But even so, he decided that it would be okay to ask Jaspierre on an actual date. He wasn't sure he could impress a beautiful woman like her, but he couldn't stop thinking about her.

Hopefully, she would consider his invitation. He looked at a couple of options downtown, even a theater. But he wanted to have dinner in a way that was a little more intimate. It seemed like whenever they talked about cases, files, her daughter, and Chance, that they never talked about each other. And he would like her to ask him about himself, to be curious and interested. He hoped to intrigue her just a bit.

After a couple of hours of thinking, he

finally decided where to take her. And he hoped that she would enjoy it.

"Hey, Jaspierre," he said into his telephone. "Would you like to have dinner? I was thinking a picnic."

She grew really quiet. He heard a muffled sound in background and fear raced up his spine. "Um, when were you thinking of going?" She was a little bit breathless; maybe she was wrestling with someone or something.

"Is Chance there? Is he in your house right now? You could just say yes and I will be on my way." His heart pounded with nervousness. She sounded like she was in mid-struggle with something bigger than her. There was a crashing noise. "Are you okay, Jaspierre? Look, I'm just going to come over."

"No, hang on a second." He heard a very loud hissing noise. Like a rush of air whistling out of a balloon. And finally, she continued, "It was nothing. I was just moving some furniture. It kind of got away from me while I was on the phone."

"Okay... But what was that hissing sound?"

There was a long pause. "It..." She paused again. It seemed to him like she couldn't think of a good lie. "It... I have no idea."

"Um. Well... Are you up for dinner?"

"Okay. How about around seven?" she said.

"Great. Are you sure nothing weird is going on? Because I can come over right now." He just knew she had to be lying.

"Hey, I'm fine. See you at seven."

She was lying. But what could he do about it? Not much. He started to have second doubts about asking her out. Yes, she was gorgeous, haunted, adorable, and talented. But she had something wrong with her. And she told a lot of lies. *So, what should I do about that?* Would she ever learn to trust him? Or would this be it? Accepting that she'd lie would not be easy for this cop. He was tempted to drive over and check on her anyway.

What if she was murdering Chance right now? Would she even tell him if she did? He found himself pacing around his over-sized dining room table. He was thinking about all this crap too much. He went back into the kitchen and start working on their picnic.

Jaspierre's Last Chance

CHAPTER

TEN

Jaspierre had ordered several cords of wood that were delivered within the hour. She already had the skeletons in the fireplace under a blazing hot fire. And the man from the barn, she wheel-barrowed up the marble steps. He reminded her quite a bit of Mother. This same long trek with Mother in the wheelbarrow instead of this man. Well, Mother's head had been in her own lap since her skeleton had been decapitated. But Mother's was the only other body she had ever wheel-barrowed into the house. So many things had changed since that moment years ago when she found Mother sitting and rotting at her desk. She tried to shake off the image.

She hadn't fed Dru or talked to him since he had been locked up. She wanted to wait a little while and let him marinate. Suffer. She was dying to ask him where the bodies of Tessa and Ikali were, but she also on some level didn't want to know. What if he had eaten them? Or dumped them in the trashcan like expired fish? Let him wait it out. Torture would come soon enough. Or rather, she supposed torture had already been started. Going hungry *was* rather unpleasant. The wheelbarrow stuck on the top step and she almost dumped the man. But she managed to save him. She did notice, that despite him being much heavier than Mother, he was much easier to wheel. Probably because she was so much stronger. Her arms were strong, her legs were strong, her butt was strong. She could probably carry three or four bodies at a time if she really wanted. How long would it take to bring all those people up from the basement?

If she had a proper furnace to burn corpses in, it would make for an easy solution to her little infestation problem. Jaspierre could guess she was the only woman in the world with a house infested with circus freaks. Maybe she should just let Dru into the maze and let them take care of him. Wouldn't it be fun? *It would.* What had happened to her cars? Was there even a chance she'd see them again? Plus, she had to try to get back whatever money he still had.

Ugh, and her job. How could she get it

back? How had Dru gotten it? Her mind rattled with questions. She'd have to interrogate him soon, but not so soon that she'd lose control. It would be infuriating to kill him before she got answers. So, turning him over to be throttled to death by the freaks, as fun as it might be, was not particularly useful to her. She had been planning on starting tonight, but then Edward called just as she was interviewing the Asian man. He managed to get a good smack on her and she ended up having to gas him. She wasn't totally sure why she'd answered the phone; obviously, that was a stupid decision. And then her second mistake was agreeing to go to dinner with Edward. Why did she do that? She needed to interview Dru, get her job back, dispose of all the circus freaks, find the corpses of her cats and daughter, and kill Chance.

She certainly did not need to go out. She did not need to sit and make moony eyes at a boy. She closed her eyes for a moment. She absolutely did not need to think about how his lips got so close to hers. Who had time for all of this? *Not her.* She was a busy woman.

Would he even like her once he found out how broke she was? She doubted it. She didn't know that much about dating, but she did know that suddenly being broke couldn't possibly help. She wasn't even sure if he liked her anyway. And she was pretty sure he *didn't* want her to just outright kill Chance. Seemed to be an outrageous request to Jaspierre. He honestly expected that she would let that man live? Even Edward, the very nice man who was a cop, should know that she deserved to kill the monster who ruined everything. What do they call it in golf? A mulligan. She should have the unfathomable right to enact justice on Chance. It seemed like the only American thing to do.

Somehow, Edward just didn't seem like he would ever see it that way. What happened to him to make him so sick and twisted? She didn't understand it. Hadn't he burned corpses when he was a child? Did his parents simply hide the harsh realities of life? Was he just naive? Did he know that it was normal? Just like speeding? Or did he really have no idea? Mother had never gotten caught. Jaspierre didn't know how many people Mother had killed, but she was guessing that it would be around thirty or more. Jaspierre had now barely killed five people. Seemed like nothing in comparison. So why on earth would he make such a big deal about it? She just didn't get it.

She finally rolled the man into the fireplace and piled log after log after log on top of him. It wouldn't be enough; she'd have to burn that fire long and hot. It would take several days to burn up the rest of the skeletons and this man from the barn. She had forgotten to check the 3-D printers to see if they were done with whatever it was they were making. Maybe she should try to attach the creation to Dru? Could be fun. She hadn't done any surgeries on anyone in years. She was completely out of practice. Of course, maybe she could practice on one of those circus freaks. She wrinkled her nose. The hot smoky smell of roasted person suddenly overcame her. She didn't really want to go through that effort. She hurried upstairs; she'd hate to accidentally smell like charred human flesh on her date. As she quickly showered, she realized she hadn't slept in her house yet.

She stepped to Lucas's room and peered inside, still wrapped in a towel. He had only stayed up there a few nights, and even those nights he didn't stay much in his own bed. Yes, it seemed like this might be a good spot to sleep. The bed was not broken. The closet was small, but conveniently, she had a downsizing of her wardrobe, what with everything missing. She hung up the two bags of clothes that she had purchased. Only two pairs of high heels and one pair of slip-on flats. It was embarrassingly bare, further evidence that she was poor. Would five hundred thousand dollars be enough to cover her wardrobe? She put on the black tall stilettos and slid on her green flirty dress. Carefully, she clicked back on the little golden necklace. "*Mine Forever.*" Every time it glinted and dangled, it would remind her to kill Chance. It seemed odd to her that her breasts were so small. She had been used to massive cleavage for so many years. A hefty set of tits. It made her uncomfortable, but she supposed if she decided to stay slim that she could always sew some on the way other women did.

She hadn't purchased anything other than a simple lipstick. So she put that on, and she put in her gold hoop earrings. They weren't expensive; she didn't have the kind of money anymore to buy expensive things. Only a hundred dollars. When she was rich again, she'd toss them and get a proper thousand-dollar pair. She glanced at the clock. Six forty-five. She was pretty early.

She walked down the stairs gracefully, clicking her heels at every step. Tears welled up in her eyes; she wanted to pet Tessa and Ikali. How would she be able to sleep in this house without them in her bed? The thought was absolutely torturous. She struggled to restrain her emotions, when she saw Arnold on a ladder, dusting the chandelier. "Hi."

"One – two – three – four. I'm almost done."
He clicked his fingers with his numbers and went
back to dusting.

"What did you and Dru fight about?" she
said. "I'm going to torture him in the morning. It'd
be great to have some insight."

Arnold turned and climbed down the
ladder. "You know the bushes out front? You
hadn't been gone very long yet. Maybe six
months? And he wanted to cut them down. I
wanted to keep them because it was making me
crazy. They were so perfect. Perfectly
symmetrical, perfectly trimmed." There was a
hesitation as his fingers clicked hard and fast at
the thought of the perfect symmetry. "But he said
they represented your authority. I said I didn't
care, I just wanted it to look symmetrical. So he
cut them down. I – I just didn't handle it well. I
told him I was going to come visit you. And that's
when I woke up down in the prison."

"Wait, so you've been down there three and
a half years?"

"Yes." He looked agitated, then silently
counted with his lips clicking his fingers. "I liked
Dru before that moment. But he couldn't even
consider leaving them just to make it easier for me
to function? Just so that I could concentrate? It
was outrageous. He hated you more than he liked

me, I guess."

"That is absolutely astounding," she said, her mind whirring. How long had Dru been planning to destroy her? And why? *Why did he hate her so much?* And then the doorbell rang.

Chapter

Eleven

Jaspierre and Edward got into his car, and he started down the long country road. It was a nice fall day. The leaves were falling and changing from green to yellow to orange to dust.

"So, happy to get out of the house?" he asked.

"Yeah." She stared out the window. She was obviously thinking about something.

"Thinking about Lucille?"

"Actually, I was thinking about Tessa and Ikali. I really miss them. I thought they were going to be at the house, but they are gone." She turned and looked at him somberly.

"Ikali and Tessa. They..." He wrinkled his nose as he tried to concentrate. "...were cougars?"

"Servals. They are much smarter than cougars. Long skinny legs and a long neck. They have both stripes and spots, and can jump six feet or more. They are really amazing. I don't know how I'm going to learn to sleep without them in my bed."

"But you haven't slept with them in your bed for years. Why do you think it will be hard to sleep?" he said, completely confused.

"But now I'm home. So it's different," she said with a tinge of annoyance. "What did you bring for a picnic?"

"Well, I think we are gonna have a lot of fun. I really do," he said. "Isn't it nice to be outside?" The car rolled into a gravel parking lot. The gravel made a crunching sound under the tires. The cool air nipped at both of their noses when they got outside. He handed her a bottle of water and slipped on a backpack. "Let's go."

"We're going on a hike?"

"Sure. Why not?" he said, suddenly lunging forward and trying to catch a leaf before it hit the ground.

"I've never been on a hike in my entire life." She frowned. Her black stilettos were a terrible decision.

"Well then, we better get to it." Edward nervously grabbed her hand and pulled her forward. They walked in silence for a bit, hands still linked together. She kept looking down at it, as if her hand was completely foreign. He felt warm, but he didn't exactly make her heart pound. Wasn't that what she was supposed to feel right now?

"How much longer do you think this is going to be?" she said. She hadn't missed a step yet. But her feet were going to start hurting soon if she wasn't careful. Her stilettos kept poking into the ground, and she carefully balanced her weight on the tips of her toes.

"Oh, I think just a bit further." They rounded a bend and came upon a little waterfall. It made a loud slushing noise. Jaspierre grinned and stuck her fingers in the water. It was cold as ice. A light shiver danced up her spine. She should've brought a sweater or something. The thin green dress was no protection from the chill. She had gotten ready for a date, not a hike.

He saw her shiver and almost wrapped his arms tight around her. But he hesitated and became too nervous. So instead, he spread the blanket on the ground. "Come have a seat."

She sat down, not too close and not too far from him. He opened the pack and pulled out hot cocoa and a long sub sandwich. They sat together quietly, and her mind kept wandering back to her servals. Should she get more servals? She wasn't sure she had time for little infant servals quite now; they were extremely demanding. And if she didn't raise them herself, they'd end up too wild. It wouldn't be worth it to have them at all. Perhaps after Chance was dead. Edward kept looking over at her, smiling awkwardly between bites.

How should she start with Dru? Maybe cut his toes off. Seemed like that had been a little overdone, but maybe it hadn't? Hard to tell. The sandwich was all right; a little heavy on the mayo. Edward scooted closer to her. A yellow leaf suddenly fell between them, landing on the plate containing the sandwich. She reached forward to grab it, and her fingertips ran into his as he reached at the same moment. Their eyes connected, and he swallowed nervously. She was frozen in time, all of her problems suddenly slipping away. Her heart pounded and her cheeks grew rosy. He leaned close, and she stared at him, seemingly noticing for the first time how much he wanted her.

He pressed his forehead against her, and just before their lips touched, the hot cocoa dumped onto his lap. He leapt back unexpectedly. She blushed and couldn't look him in the eye. He didn't try to kiss her again, instead cleaning up the mess and laughing awkwardly. They hiked back to his car, and for the first time, he suddenly realized she was in high heels. "Oh! I can't believe you're wearing those shoes. I, I should have realized. I am *so* sorry."

"I had fun." She leaned her back against the car while he put his backpack in the trunk. He closed it, and suddenly, they were standing close again. She reached her fingertips out and adjusted his collar. Any second now she was going to kiss him, pull him tight, and let her lips do the talking. But he was still soaked from cocoa, and he nervously pulled away, opening her door. She got in and they rode back quietly. He was grinning the entire time. She couldn't figure out why it was so hard to kiss him.

Eventually, his fingertips found hers. And they both, like smiling idiots, said nothing until they got to her house. "Well?" he said. He seemed to be trying to think of something further to say.

"Good night, I guess." She got out of the car and closed the door. Her heels starting to click up the marble steps. She didn't know how dates normally ended; she hadn't been on a proper date in a very, very long time. He leapt out of the car and raced up the steps, grabbing her hand. His other hand slid behind her back, pressing her waist to his. He was breathless, and she suddenly was breathless too.

He leaned in close and pressed his lips to

her ear. "I have to kiss you good night." And then he did. His lips caught hers with magic intensity and everything she knew stopped and started all over again. Her whole body trembled with delight, ecstasy running through her. As soon as he released her, her knees dropped out from under her, and he had to catch her. She was so red and flustered that she couldn't figure out anything to say. So she rushed inside, closing the door and leaning against it. Her heart was pounding and her breath was short. She had certainly never been kissed like that before.

CHAPTER

TWELVE

The man from the barn was roasting. The smell permeated the house, despite the wide-open dampers. Jaspierre couldn't wait until all she could smell was wood ash. His skin was charred, and his meat was probably about cooked through. He needed at least a few more days before he would turn to ash. The other bones hadn't gotten the least bit brittle. This fire was certainly not hot enough. She threw on a ton more wood, pumping the bellows so the fire would get hotter and hotter. Then she clicked the broken serval's ear, and the entire fireplace, fire and all, slid. She'd have to shut the door quickly, or the fire would suffocate. She traipsed down the stairs and shut the door behind her.

Edward had kissed her. She closed her eyes for a moment and let her body deliciously remember how her knees grew weak. How the entire world stopped and held its breath until they parted. *How he kissed her very soul!* And then, with that done, she wrenched it from her mind and got to work. *Things to do, people to kill, Dru to torture.*

The people in the maze, the circus freaks, were generally being polite to each other. They sat in small groups, quietly talking. She didn't bother listening in, what could they possibly say that would be interesting? The Asian man was still unconscious, and the red-haired girl was sleeping on a cot. Dru was pouting.

She slipped on a headset, pressing several buttons, until he could hear her and she could hear him. "Dru?" She grinned and pressed the button, spraying him down. She pressed another and the spray stopped, "Dru. I want to know what happened to Tessa and Ikali."

He tried to answer, but she soaked him again. "Dru. I want to know what happened to Tessa and Ikali."

"Fuck —" Water soaked him a third time. He had barely even finished the whole word. *Was he stupid? Was there something wrong with him? Had he gone mental?* He would answer her soon enough. She pressed another button; gas soaked into his room. He was unconscious very quickly. She held her hand against the smooth, long wall, and the door slid open. She went down the metal spiral staircase and looked at the smooth white hallway. It had been quite some time since she had been down here.

She found her mind wandering to the first time she walked into Lucas's room and tore off her own panties. It had been incredible. But he didn't kiss like Edward. Lucas loved her because he had to. There was no one else. But Edward, he wanted to kiss her for no reason at all. It was absolutely astounding. Edward didn't get anything from kissing her besides... the kiss.

She slipped her hand onto the cold white wall and held it. The door in front of her slid open. Dru was lying completely unconscious on the floor. She pressed her hand onto the wall in his room, and the little dumbwaiter opened. She clicked the long metal ring around his waist and climbed the ring ladder on the wall. At the very top, she dropped the chain through the loop. At the bottom, she connected it to Dru's waist. The other end of the chain she clicked to the bottom ring on the wall. Not too shabby. She needed to move him closer to get it all the way set up.

She picked up his unconscious body pushed him tight against the wall between the two rings. Then she grabbed the end of the chain and held it as hard as she could until his back rose into the air. She clicked the chain into the bottom loop again, locking it in place. In the same manner, she fastened a chain to each of his hands and feet, with the chains looping high into the loops up above, and locked on the bottom rings. With this setup, she could allow him freedom to move or dangle him in any position she desired. Most importantly, he couldn't easily swing his fists at her unless she let him.

She had a vague curiosity if she would want to have sex with him. She hadn't had sex since Lucas, not anyone special before him. Almost five years ago. Dru couldn't do anything if she decided to have sex with him. He couldn't do anything if she decided not to. She looked at him but felt nothing, so she slapped him hard. And he started to wake up. He tried to swing at her with his fist, but he couldn't quite reach her. She grabbed the chain looped around his waist and gave it hard yank, hoisting him up farther. He let out a yelp.

"Dru. I want to know what happened to Tessa and Ikali." He was now dangling, his feet about at her shoulder level. He tried to kick her, but the chain on his foot was too short.

"Dru. I want to know what happened to Tessa and Ikali." Maybe she needed to get laid. It'd been a lot of years, and she'd been under a lot of stress. She should just go make out with Edward. Why would she have sex with Dru? She was probably just getting excited because she was remembering Lucas. Gorgeous Lucas and his soft body. *God, Lucas was amazing.* What kind of luck would she have at getting that again? Her odds were probably pretty lousy. "Dru. I want to know what happened to Tessa and Ikali." She sneered, looking at his angry face.

"Fuck you."

"Dru." She yanked the chain as hard as she could, and his ass rose into the air. It looked like the wind was knocked from him. "I want to know what happened to Tessa and Ikali." She let go of the chain, and he fell suddenly. His body whooshed from above her head, back to her eye level, hovering just above the floor. He bounced at the bottom of the chain like a yo-yo.

He let out a painful moan. He was visibly gasping. He screamed, "Stop it. Stop. How do you expect me to think?"

"Dru. I want to know what happened to Tessa and Ikali!" She grabbed the chain, yanking it, then releasing, dropping him again. This fall wasn't as far, but it got the message across. If he fucked around, she'd drop him again. "You said that you had them. You promised to take care of them! What the fuck happened to Tessa and

Ikali?"

He hung limply. For a moment, she worried that maybe he was unconscious. What a fucking waste of the day if he couldn't stay alert and stay awake. She could feel her heart pounding harder and harder and, for a moment, she wished she had a blade. She was lusting for him to die. This fucking monster took her money, her job, her servals. But she couldn't allow herself that luxury. If she had a blade, he'd never last long enough to tell her where Tessa and Ikali were. If she had a blade, he wouldn't make it until morning. He wouldn't make it another hour, he wouldn't make it another moment. *No, no blades.* This was one of the ways she would control herself.

"Dru, I want to know. What happened to Tessa and Ikali?" Her voice was steady, despite her rage, starting to build and roar inside her belly.

He raised his head very slowly; he was gasping harder. He had tears in his eyes. "I got rid of them." And he smiled. His teeth were tinted with blood.

"You fucking animal." She gripped the chain with both hands, swinging her weight against it. He rose in the air as she released and he fell. And again, she threw her weight against the chain, raising him up like a flag at the pole. Then she dropped him as easily as one would drop a bouncy ball down a flight of stairs. "Why would you kill them! Why would you do that! They were innocent." Her heart was pounding and she could only see red. She could hardly even hear his gasping cries. There was a rushing sound in her ears. And her heart hurt.

She knew, she fucking knew Tessa and Ikali had to be dead. And yet, after hearing Dru confessing that he killed them, it was still a shock. It was absolutely excruciating. Tears flooded down her face. She couldn't take it! She couldn't take another second. She grabbed the chain, screaming with rage, and climbed up, her entire body pulling the chain down. Hand over hand, foot over foot, climbing higher and higher. Dru was screaming at the top of his lungs as he flew into the air higher and higher. Her weight lifted him, and when she finally reached for the rings on the wall releasing the chain, he fell twenty feet down to the end of the chain. He gurgled, his organs smashed inside his guts. He retched blood.

"They deserved better!" She was clinging to the wall, twenty feet in the air. Slowly, she climbed down. Rage made her body tingle and tremor. "They deserved fucking better, you lying motherfucking asshole."

Her hands trembled as she grasped the

chain again. "No!" he said in a desperate wheezing cry. "Stop. Please. Please stop. I didn't kill them." He coughed a blood spatter on the white crisp floor. He was gasping, and tears and blood were running down his face. "I didn't kill them. I got rid of them." Vomit flowed out his mouth. He cried, gasping for air.

Her eyes grew wide with surprise. She could get them back! "Where did you send them? What happened to Ikali and Tessa! Where are they?" Her heart was pounding, and she was unbearably excited. He better tell her soon.

"Let me out. Let me out, then I'll tell you." He sniffled, gasping again. His body was shuddering with pain.

She smiled, both hands on the chain. "You fucking idiot." And she pulled him up and dropped him again. He screamed, flailing, trying to brace himself. And after he hit the bottom, he passed out. She left him dangling and trudged upstairs, humming merrily.

* * * * * * * * * * * *

Chance was nine hours into the drive when he stopped for his first piss. He was still kicking himself for missing her release, but excitement grew as the miles flew past. He stopped at a 7-Eleven. He walked inside after he emptied his kidneys in the dirty bathroom stall. He picked up a couple candy bars, two Gatorades, and a Monster energy drink. While he was standing at the checkout waiting for the gas attendant to finally notice him, he saw a newspaper sitting on the counter.

The front-page header had her name splashed across it. Jaspierre – heiress, mother, murderer--released. It had a picture of her mug shot on the day her baby was born. On the day Lucille was born. Her wild, almost drugged eyes were intoxicating.

Chance didn't like to think of her like that. Had she gotten fat wallowing in her cell? Or was she her *normal* plump self? Maybe she'd made it to 300 pounds. He grinned. He had certainly put on a few pounds himself. He liked to consider himself well rounded, waiting for her. Maybe her body would smash him into the mattress when they fucked. Finally, the sales lady turned around and let out a scream with her eyes. They were wide and bulging. Her fingertips went to her lips, holding back any actual sound. After a moment, she regained her composure and quickly scanned his items.

Chance grinned; all those tattoos and scars were still so beautiful after all these years. He never even needed to retouch them. Because they were just so effective. People would cringe when they saw him, *and they should cringe*. He was one terrifying bastard. They should be straight up frightened. At one point a few years ago, he considered counting up how many people he killed. He lost track somewhere around a hundred, and what he found was he didn't actually care.

He handed the nervous cashier some cash, his eyes still not leaving Jaspierre's frightened mug shot. She was truly beautiful; she could've been a model if she wanted that kind of life. Or perhaps an actress. Although being a dreamily rich heiress was pretty damn good too. He thought about Lucille and Peter. But before he got very far, the lady handed him a pile of ones. Fourteen of them, to be exact. "What the hell? Do you have any tens? Or fives?" A bite of anger curled up his throat. Why would this bitch give him a pile of ones like he was some sort of stripper? The lady didn't even reply; she just backed up.

"It's the middle of the fucking day. How can you not have any fives or tens?" He slammed his fist on the counter this time. Ten minutes later, he left the gas station with all the cash from the cash register stuffed in his pockets, and her broken body slumped on the floor.

Twenty hours to go.

CHAPTER

THIRTEEN

Jaspierre waited what felt like an eternity, but in reality was about an hour, for Dru to wake up. During that hour, she paced uncomfortably in her control room. She stared at the circus freaks huddled nervously around each other. She found herself doing push-ups, sit-ups, and anything else she could think of. Fucking asshole passed out. Where the hell were Tessa and Ikali? They had to be dead. Dru had shown her pictures throughout the years about how well they were doing. When had he given them up? No one would take in servals and even if they did, they would not know how to take care of them. Absolutely outrageous, the thought of her cats sitting with some other incapable, poor owner.

Speaking of being poor, she ran her bank account numbers across her mind. Ten more pushups, this time one-handed. It hadn't been long, but surely her office would want to know why their precious CEO had vanished.

She had made too many mistakes, one after another. When she first went to trial, she relied on Dru; he seemed so warm and helpful in that first year. He promised Tessa and Ikali were well taken care of, and even brought pictures once a month. He showed up religiously on Sundays as though she was some sort of church. He'd listen to her incoherent ramblings, and he would reassure her.

Reassure her about anything and everything. He promised he had an investigator searching for Lucille. *He promised.* He promised her servals were safe and happy and well fed. He promised her business was being well looked after and brought her notes.

But slowly, his visits faded from weekly to monthly, and then in the last six months, she had barely seen him at all.

She had gotten a bit worried but not as alarmed as she should have been. He explained he was busy, and things were well. She worried a bit that he was mismanaging things, or had grown disinterested in her, but she had no idea it had gotten to this point. That it had shifted from minor mismanagement to absolute thievery. Had there ever been an investigator? How many checks had she written to the man for stuff that never existed?

Had the cats been fed? How many checks had she written to take care of them? And how exactly was the rest of the money in her accounts emptied? Even with all the checks she had written for thousands upon thousands, her account had been positively bursting at the seams when she went to prison.

What had happened to the ruppies? They were Mother's work--part dog, part rabbit. Beautiful creations. He had been giving reports on how well they had done. Four ruppies, each with lovely names: Sarah, Kurt, Beyonce, and Toto. She had *pictures*, she had names, and reports on their growth.

As she considered these things, she remembered that the reports had been written in Arnold's peculiar handwriting. The way he carefully crossed his Zs right in the middle with a perfect dash. She would have to ask him how they got the pictures. It was so hard after all these years to watch everything crumbling before her eyes. She should have known better; she should have realized that he was destroying her.

Lucille had been killed by Chance. What would Lucille think to know that Jaspierre had done nothing to find her? She "thought" she had done something, but she had done nothing. It was horrifying. Jasp paused mid pushup to swallow back the bile that was forming in her throat. The panicky feeling that made her want to claw her own skin off her body was peppering at the back of her mind.

Mother was strong, brilliant, and, dare she say it, evil. Jaspierre had vowed to do better for her daughter and in fact she had done worse than any mother had ever done. Lucille had been snatched from her mere moments after her birth. How could this be? How could she have let this be?

Her mind whirled back to her missing servals. They were her constant comfort. Even in prison, she was convinced that they would be there for her. She called their names in her sleep. Her safest thought was that she had not lost everything. She had two precious pieces of her family left.

And it turned out to be a lie. They were gone, *they were gone.* Dead or mutilated. Someone probably skinned them just for a bit of fur. Nobody could have possibly loved them like she did. She found herself gasping with hysterical sobs. How could being out feel so horrible? *How dare it be so horrible?*

Her terrible sobs were broken by a laugh. Not her laugh; Dru's laugh. "Are you crying?" he said, still her puppet in his cell. "You're crying!" He laughed harder.

That fucking bastard. She pulled from the console slot a long sharp blade. Fuck him and all his fucking shit.

She stormed down the spiral staircase into the smooth hallway. Her hand pressed tightly to the wall, warming it slightly until the door slid open. Dru hung like a retired marionette, his limbs limp. His mouth still dripped with blood.

She pressed the tip of the blade to his forehead and lifted his sagging head to look at hers. Her tears were still wet on her cheeks. "Dru. I want to know what happened to Tessa and Ikali."

"I bet you do. You are just like her, you know? Just like Severina. You deserve every fucking bit of trouble you get yourself into," he seethed at her, his head barely able to hold itself up. He tried to pull back so the blade wouldn't cut, but the blade slipped through his skin, tapping at his skull.

"Don't talk about Mother!" she screamed. It was so desperately difficult to keep the blade from leaping to his stomach, pulling his guts open. It begged her, it demanded her. It needed to bite into his flesh, deeper. Her fingertips gripped the blade tightly, begging it to wait, wait until she knew where her precious pets were. Trembling, she said, "Dru. I want to know what happened to Tessa and Ikali." Her voice grew fierce with each repeated word.

"Severina never had an attachment to pets. She never had an attachment to you either. She said we should skin you and see if you were as shitty on the inside as you were on the outside."

Jaspierre gasped. Not because he said Mother threatened to skin her. Mother threatened a great many things and it wasn't a surprise to Jaspierre in the least. She was shocked because he said *we*. *We should skin you*. It began to register in her mind that he knew Mother, like he really knew her, not a little but a lot.

"Mother?" She couldn't seem to say anything else. The word lingered on her lips, and the tip of her sword lowered in surprise.

"Severina. Your mother. My lover."

"She fucked a lot of men, so I wouldn't exactly say that means anything," Jaspierre snorted back. But she was still uncertainly holding the blade.

"Severina was my wife." All the blood rushed to Jaspierre's ears, and she couldn't hear anything. Her face grew hot and red. His wife? Mother had been married?

Chapter

Fourteen

"You couldn't have been married to Mother," Jaspierre said, but the confidence in her voice suddenly faded. How could she possibly know that?

"I was married to Severina." He smiled a bloody smile, coughing slightly so little flecks of blood flew into the air.

"I don't believe you!" Jaspierre shouted, dropping the blade and reaching for the chain.

"I knew Jasper! I knew Pierre. I helped her build this very room. It used to be accessed by a door in her bedroom!" He suddenly was shouting too. Her fingertips lingered on the chain, ready to hoist him up and drop him like a hot potato.

"I don't believe you," Jaspierre said quietly, tears forming in her eyes, threatening to spill over. How could he know Mother? How could she have been married? "You liar." Her voice grew low and hateful.

"I'm not lying! It's true. I can tell you all about her. I can tell you everything you've wanted to know." His eyes connected with hers and, for a painful moment, she remembered she had thought about having sex with this man. With this same man Mother fucked. Her hands trembled, but that flash of anger spurred her to action.

She threw her weight into the chain and he let out a scream of protest before he fell. His body flopped at the end with a nasty thwack. "Dru. I want to know what happened to Tessa and Ikali." Her head was screaming *Mother*. The thumping in her head grew loud and she knew it was her heart. Sweat was forming on her back. *How could he know Mother!* A scream burrowed within her chest. The urge to tear away at her skin with her fingertips grew so strong that her right hand twitched.

"What happened to Tessa and Ikali!" she shouted, ignoring Mother. *Avoiding her.* It reminded her of one night when she was a little girl and she tried, she desperately tried to get a drink of water without Mother finding out. Tiptoed to the kitchen, carefully climbed the counter, gently lifted a glass. Pausing every breath to listen. And Mother somehow was there. She was there in the kitchen, watching Jaspierre. She waited for her to be precariously balanced, holding that glass, sneaking to the sink. She waited. And then she struck, her pointed stiletto piercing her skin. How had Jaspierre missed her? She had scanned the room. She had been as silent as a fairy. Mother seemed to just be. She defied all logic. Somehow she was in that room again, sneaking for water, Mother lurking nearby, waiting to strike.

"Where are they? You will tell me!" She threw her weight into the chain again, lifting him up, and he started to beg. But it was too little too late, and he crashed back down the end of his string. *Dance, you motherfucking marionette.*

"Stop," he whimpered, tears running down his face. "Please, please. I'll tell you. Just let me go."

"Wrong answer, fuck-face." She leaned into the chain again.

"No!" he shouted, gasping with pain. "They are at the zoo! Stop, please. *Don't!*" He let out a soft scream as he fell back down, the chain snagging around his belly, blood coughing out his mouth. He was still weeping loudly when she closed the fireplace shut.

She shuddered, her body trembling with adrenaline. Dru could not know Mother. She was running, through her office, through the foyer. He could not. She faltered on the stairs, tripping and slamming into a step. Letting out a shout, she raced to the shower.

Her fingertips scrubbed at her skin, the hot water steaming the glass. She couldn't breath. She grew frantic, scrubbing harder and harder. How dare he lie to her. How dare he say he knew Mother. Gasping for air. He could not possibly have married her! The scrubbing turned into clawing; long scratches grew dark red on her arms.

No.

She gritted her teeth and resisted the urge to continue. *Go find Tessa and Ikali. You'll feel much better.*

Her hands trembled as she turned off the water. The desire to scratch was so strong. Mother fucked everyone up. Still naked and dripping, she morphed the energy into pushups, one after another until she was winded and sore, and yet she pressed on. The frantic pace hurt, but she kept at it until her body collapsed underneath her. And then, she cried.

Her desperate clinging to Tessa and Ikali dulled the pain of the loss of Lucille. The deep, unrelenting pain. She was alone. Mother was dead, Lucas was dead, Lucille was surely dead. All she had was her servals, Tessa and Ikali, and even they could be dead.

She rummaged through her few outfits, finally slipping on the grey t-shirt dress. Her arms were like Jell-O, weak from the effort of the pushups. She restlessly slept a few hours on the bed, and at six in the morning she awoke, ready to go. Slowly, she went downstairs, grabbed an apple, and ate it while she walked to her car. Time to go to the zoo.

The car purred beneath her foot, and she sped off to get her babies back.

Jaspierre's Last Chance

Chapter

Fifteen

Jaspierre stood staring into the serval pen. There was only one serval in the pen. It did not look up at her. She wasn't sure if it was Ikali or Tessa or some other serval. It would not look up at her. She couldn't bring herself to call out either of their names and instead just stared at the miserable cat.

The pen didn't seem nearly large enough. There were no waterfalls and just a small bowl of dry food sitting in the corner. The serval looked thin and miserable, lifeless almost. Most certainly it hadn't chased a mouse or rabbit or squirrel in years. The way it was sitting, curled up, with its back to her, she wondered if it was sickly. Maybe it was tired of being looked at.

She stared at the pen. It was an open pen with a long drop into the cage. But the edge was a fence, then a concrete fall guard, then much father down was the grass area for the servals. Thirty feet? Fifty feet? She wasn't sure.

Which one was it? Tessa or Ikali?

Hot shame ran across her face. Shouldn't she be able to tell? She had slept with them in her bed for years, she had fed them when they were babies. Why couldn't she recognize the backside of her pet?

She whispered, "Tessa?" And clicked her tongue a few times. "Tessa? Ikali?"

The serval's ear twitched, but it didn't lift its head.

"Tessa?" she said a bit louder. The ear twitched again. "Ikali?"

In a remarkably slow manner, the cat yawned and stretched, butt in the air towards Jaspierre. "Psst," she hissed at it. "Tessa? Ikali?"

Finally, the cat turned around. Its long striped and spotted body looked lean. There was a large patch of fur missing from its belly. Jaspierre's eyes narrowed in irritation. Was it sick?

The serval looked at her, and she at it. Recognition hit her immediately. "Ikali!" she shouted, startling the family next to her. He let out a growl and sniffed the air. "Ikali?" she said back with a whisper. He started pacing anxiously, letting out a yowling meow. *Shit*. She had upset him. He wanted out, and he wanted out now.

He quickly grew frantic, howling at the top of his lungs, pacing back and forth, running in circles. The idiot attendees of the zoo took pictures and commented on how pretty he was. He was thin, sickly, missing fur, and howling in anger, and they were taking pictures! She gripped the railing tightly, completely furious. Where was Tessa? What happened to her? Ikali was increasingly upset until a zoo official came over. He tossed a raw piece of meat, but Ikali ignored it, hissing loudly. He violently charged the zookeeper and ended up with a loud thwacking crack at his skull. The zookeeper had a long metal prod he slapped Ikali with. The cat backed up, growling and howling. A large crowd was gathering. Ikali was hissing and the zookeeper prodded him with the stick, pushing him towards a metal door. The cat tried to fight but visibly gave up after a loud shocking zap. He slinked, his tail between his legs, into the small door. A few minutes later, a different serval slipped out another door. This one was young and wrestled a little toy ball.

Could Tessa be inside?

Jaspierre slowly counted to ten, her heart still beating up her throat. How could they treat her gorgeous family this way? Once she had control of herself, she walked to the building attached to the serval pen. There was a viewing room inside. She entered and in the crowd of guests, she saw several small glass pens. In the center of the room was Tessa on a leash. The demonstrator made her leap up and catch a toy he tossed. Tessa's ears perked up and her eyes snapped to Jaspierre. She let out a long hissing sound and prowled forward. She looked angry and hurt.

Jaspierre stepped closer into the audience sitting around the platform. The zookeeper yanked the chain on Tessa's neck, and she turned and hissed at him. Her large paw shot out and swiped, tearing at his leg. Tessa was going frantic, suddenly wrestling at the end of the leash. Her teeth bared, and her long sharp claws swiped harder at the zookeeper. His leg was gushing. He couldn't control her. Two more zookeepers suddenly showed up, and a security guard started ushering the audience out the door. Jaspierre found herself pressed against a wall, trying not to be swept up in the tide of people frantically hiding their children's eyes from the gore. Tessa was surrounded.

"What the hell? She's always been so docile!" She hissed again at the man on the end of her leash; he was whimpering and blood was dripping off his shoe. She leapt on him, biting his neck. Jaspierre couldn't help but grin. Tessa, beautiful Tessa, was taking down her captor. Frantically, one zookeeper tried to pull her off the man she was slaughtering. The other one pulled out a large taser, barbed and angry on the end of the stick. The room was clearing even faster now. Screaming children grew quieter as their parents dragged them out of the room. The security guard finally noticed Jaspierre and started to walk towards her. He kept pointing at her, then pointing at the door.

Tessa let out a loud yowling cry of pain as the taser sharply crackled in her skin. She turned and swiped the knees of the man. The zookeeper under her was already dead, blood still gushing. She was so focused on the one with the taser that she missed the zookeeper on the other side, yanking her chain, cracking a long stick at her. Jaspierre's eyes connected with Tessa's as she let out another cry of pain. Could she have cried "help me" any louder?

Now. It was now. No planning, just get her cats home.

Jaspierre's blade practically flew to her hand and quickly gutted the security guard. The room was empty of visitors at this point. He barely even gargled a reply as his body spilled open. Tessa let out another cry as one zookeeper yanked on her and the other shocked her repeatedly. Jaspierre charged and the man with the taser was quickly skewered. The other zookeeper let out a terrified cry. The blade swished and, with a quick slice to his throat, it was over. Tessa snarled and bared her teeth at Jaspierre.

They stood on the center stage, three zookeepers in their brown-turning-red uniforms littering the floor around them. Tessa hissed, her tail flicking back and forth anxiously. "Tessa. We've got to get Ikali. Calm down."

Tessa lunged for her, teeth snapping together violently just inches from her face. Her sharp claws raked down Jaspierre's arm. The chain around her neck was still wrapped around a dead man, slowing her down. Bright red blood ran down Jaspierre's arm as she stared at Tessa, considering.

She's gone wild.

Jaspierre turned and tried the service door next to the bathroom. It was locked. She quickly ran back to the stage and rifled through the dead man's pockets. She found the keys soon enough, leaving Tessa still tied to the dead man to wait. Hot, hateful growls came from the serval, but her frantic pacing slowed.

"Settle down, baby. We're gonna get out of here."

It was lucky that nobody was in the back room, or security would have already descended upon this little display. Jaspierre picked up one of the long taser rods and carefully read all the cage levers. She propped open the service door with a manual she found. Then she opened each line of cages and their doors. Slowly, the first serval walked out.

It was a young serval and very angry, hissing at Jaspierre and threatening to bite her. Jaspierre waved the taser mildly, and the serval exited into the stage area. Four more servals slowly exited to the stage area. Each looked angry and hateful, threatening Jaspierre. Ikali was the last one to come out. It struck her suddenly how old he looked. His whiskers had greyed. He should be pleasantly enjoying retirement. Her heart ached for him.

She stepped back as he walked past her. He never even looked her way. A small kitten serval meowed from a crate in the back. She walked back and looked and found three little kittens, two sleeping, one crying. *Fucking shit.* What exactly was her plan?

There was a backpack on the floor filled with schoolbooks. Perhaps it was a lost and found item, but it served her purposes just fine. She dumped the contents and stuffed the three kittens inside along with as many bottles as she could fit. They were squished, but it would only be for a moment. This scouting run had changed into a rescue mission. How the hell was she going to get them out of here? They couldn't possibly even fit in her car; she just had that Lexus.

She wasn't even sure if it had a back seat.

There was a stack of leashes on hooks, and she quickly grabbed them. In the main room, all the servals were hissing at each other, tails flickering, pacing anxiously. A few zoo visitors were looking in the big glass door, uncertain if they could come in. Jaspierre shook her head at them, but they kept watching as she approached her two pets. Tessa was still chained to the dead man. Jaspierre quickly leashed her, trying to keep clear of her angry claws. Tessa was calmer, though, and didn't bother biting.

Tessa's mouth was grey and she was thin with age. Jaspierre, even with all this going on, felt a pang of worry. How much longer would they even have? She leashed Ikali, who was calm, but seemed not to recognize her anymore. There were now five servals off leash. One was not fully grown, but big. The other four were fully grown, but not as old as Ikali and Tessa. One female looked pregnant, and another still had wet teats. She was the mother of the three in the backpack most likely. After a moment's decision, she came up with her plan and leashed all of the cats. They would be nearly impossible to control, but that wasn't the point. She pressed onward, pulling the unruly cats towards the door. They hissed at each other, and she got a painful swipe of claws scraping across her legs. She opened the door and released one of the older servals. It immediately started running down the path between visitors, hissing and swiping. Screaming and running ensued, and as something startled the serval, she saw it pop upwards eight feet or so, and then disappear from view. She released two more quickly, leashes trailing behind them. The path was clearing extremely fast, and visitors were scrambling to hide their children and run for their lives.

It was an idiotic notion; the servals were trying to leave, not hunt, but visitors were idiots, so they ran screaming towards the exit. She only had four left: Tessa, Ikali, the young one, and the pregnant one.

This seemed to her to be a manageable number, and she quickly pushed them all out the door. Tessa and Ikali walked along just fine on the leash. They had been walking on leash together for their entire lives. Quickly, they fell into a smooth rhythm, as fast as Jaspierre could run. The teenage serval kept horsing around; he'd barely been on a leash and he'd never seen the world. Distraction was his middle name.

The pregnant one was terrified, hissing and trying to duck behind a bush, or dart up a tree over and over. But Tessa, Ikali, and Jaspierre pushed on, pulling the ragtag two with them. The zoo was cleared in front of them and behind them, they suddenly heard a security man in a golf cart. "What the fuck are you doing!?" He was screaming at her, and the soft whirring of the cart grew to a steady hum.

Jaspierre kept running as fast as her feet would allow. Thank God she was so fit. Her heart couldn't have done this before, but it would do it now. Her lungs burned with a fiery heat, a stitch growing more and more painful in her side. The parking lot, if she could make it to the parking lot, she'd be fine. The pregnant one suddenly let out a screaming yowl and pulled hard to the right; she needed to hide, she desperately needed to hide. Jaspierre released her and she scrambled up a tall tree. Jaspierre felt small claws digging painfully into her back as the three baby servals cried loudly, scared and clawing to get out. The security guard leapt from his cart. He screamed, "Shut the gate" into a little walkie-talkie. He ran fast, not nearly as winded as Jaspierre, and turned to grab her, but she didn't have to fight him at all. The teenage serval swiped the guard, ripping into his legs and the man faltered and screamed. He fell, grasping both bleeding legs.

They continued to run, with Tessa on one side of the teen and Ikali on the other. They pushed him along, keeping his distractions to a minimum. Jaspierre could see the main gates ahead of her. One of the baby servals tore a hole in the backpack, and his yowls grew much, much louder with his tiny mouth pressed to the hole.

The gate was crowded with terrified guests leaving en masse. Screaming ensued and people trampled people, running from Jaspierre and her angry servals. There wasn't really a path, but people ran, and the teen clawed and bit at everyone he could reach. Tessa and Ikali let out some halfhearted swipes, but they seemed mostly winded and tired. *And old.* They seemed so old.

The baby serval cried loudly again and Jaspierre saw the crowd of people react. She tried to run for the car, but teeth, big angry teeth caught her calf. *The mother had come.*

Screaming, Jaspierre swirled and kicked the angry serval mother. The leash was still dangling from her neck. Jaspierre screamed, "Come on! We must run," pleading with the cat. Tessa suddenly let out a loud hiss, impatient to continue. The teen and Ikali were pulling at the leash, trying to escape into the parking lot, into the world. Jaspierre scrambled and security people were racing towards her. She grabbed the mother's leash and screamed again, "Run! We must run!"

And suddenly, the mother joined them and they raced to the parking lot. A fat woman was standing at the back of her minivan, unloading two small children from a stroller. The minivan was running and the sliding door was open. Jaspierre launched herself inside, dragging the unruly servals. Quickly, she slammed the door shut. The fat woman at the back of the minivan started to shout something, but the teen bared his teeth from inside the van and looked ready to pounce. She slammed the back of the door down sharply, just as Jaspierre managed to hit the gas. They flew down the road at an incredible speed. Jaspierre was panting and still surged with adrenaline. The kittens tumbled out of the backpack, the mother frantically helpedto dig them out. Jaspierre did a quick head count as she swerved onto the highway; Tessa, Ikali, three kittens, Mother, and Teen. Seven, seven wild servals in her car. She glanced into the rear-view mirror. Mother was licking her kittens and hiding

them in the back seat. Tessa and Ikali were
snuggled up close, sleeping already. But Teen, he
was licking his teeth angrily, tail flickering and
eying her.

He was going to bite her soon. These were
wild cats. Not pets; wild cats. Wild.

They could kill her.

She tried not to focus on that, instead
focusing on getting home so she could put them in
the maze and figure out how to tame them.

Shit. Those circus freaks were still in there.
Fuck.

Her mind whirled as she tried to decide
what to do. She cracked the window a bit and
Teen was suddenly distracted by the smells, his
nose pressed tight to the gap as he stared at the
world flying by. Thank God for that bit of luck.

She'd have to release them in the house.

Perhaps they'd kill her when she was
changing her clothes.

Perhaps they'd settle in nicely.

Fuck, she didn't even have any cat food or
mice. Why the fuck didn't she plan ahead more?
Where could she stash wild cats? Where could she
lose this minivan? *Fuck, fuck, fuck*.

Loud police sirens started up behind her.
They had a ways to go, but they would catch her.
Fuck.

Jaspierre's Last Chance

CHAPTER

SIXTEEN

Jaspierre pulled off the main road into a smaller neighborhood. If she was even the least bit lucky, she would be able to wait for the police to pass and then she could hop back on the road and get to her house.

The teen started wrestling with one of the kittens, and Jaspierre glanced back at them. Ikali and Tessa had fallen asleep, the mother was nursing the other two kittens. It seemed things had settled for a moment. Where the hell could she put these servals? Tessa and Ikali could stay in the house, but there was a real risk Mother, Teen, and the kittens would end up too wild to keep indoors. They needed constant handling to tame them, and that was nearly impossible when they could escape to any portion of a mansion.

She pulled into a quiet dead end and

parked. Sirens whirred past. She needed to change her plates. It was pretty easy these days to send out a massive text to everyone and the whole road would have eyes on your car. Every person in her city would have a flashing warning: *Find this minivan, find it!*

She didn't have a screwdriver, though, and it was pretty difficult to change plates without one. However, there was always the poor persons' way of obscuring it. If she had a marker, she could scribble a number just enough to look like another. But she didn't carry a marker around. Perhaps she should get one just for this purpose.

Plus, she left her Lexus behind. She'd have to go get it.

Instead, she'd have to do it a different way. She stepped out of the car quickly and glanced around. She didn't see anyone, so she quickly picked up a muddy clot of dirt and pressed it tightly into the plate. It seemed to stick, and five minutes later, the plate was coated in mud, and the car had several clots on the back. She smeared as much mud as she could stand on the vehicle so that it wouldn't be too suspicious that the plate was caked in the stuff. Thankfully, this minivan hadn't been washed in years, as far as she could tell, so adding a couple of bucketsful of mud wasn't that big of a deal. Her hands were filthy, though. As she climbed back into the minivan, she wiped her filthy mud crusted hands on the passenger seat.

Good enough.

She pulled back onto the main road, slowly driving back to her mansion. Once she arrived, she left the servals in the minivan while she went in. "Arnold?" she shouted. "Arnold? I need some help. I've got Ikali and Tessa, and a few others, but I need..." Her voice caught in her throat as Arnold walked into the front room from the kitchen. He was bleeding from his eye socket, and his left arm hung limply at his side. His right arm was twisted painfully behind his back.

Chance held that arm, smiling cruelly at Jaspierre. "Hello, honey, I'm home."

* * * * * * * * * * * *

"Hello Chance," Jaspierre said, and her fingers seemed to twitch. Where was her nearest blade? The stair banister, if Dru hadn't taken it and lost it. She raised both hands up in a surrender fashion.

"I've missed you." His eyes were lingering on her body, not her face.

Her heart flipped. "Lucille?" She could barely croak out her name suddenly. She didn't want to hear it, to hear of her death. But she had to know. "Lucille?" she tried again, desperately trying to hold it together.

Arnold let out a moan as Chance twisted his arm harder. "What do you want me to do with him?"

"Arnold, I have my cats in my car. Please put them in..." She hesitated before she came up with a plan. "You know the playroom? With the ladders and what not? They are leashed. Carefully lead them in there and shut the door. They will need to be fed."

Chance wrinkled his brow; it wasn't exactly his style to let a man just wander off. But he didn't give a shit about Arnold. He could kill him later if it came to that. His grip relaxed and Arnold slipped free quickly, hesitating at the front door.

"Hurry up. They are hungry," she said, her eyes never leaving Chance. "Lucille." This time, her voice was strong and firm. He was staring at her body again.

"You've gotten thin," he said plainly. "Your tits are way smaller."

"Lucille," she said louder, suddenly striding to the banister. The sword was still there, sliding out with a sharp whistle. "Lucille, God help you, *Lucille!*" Her voice was rattling with rage. The blade's tip skittered loudly across the floor as she slowly and deliberately raised it to his throat.

"Hey now. I am sorry I didn't know you got

out. You weren't supposed to be out for a few
more years. Years, you know? I've been up in
Canada, and I'm sorry I missed it. I'd be pissed
too." He didn't even put his hands up, but instead
held them out, offering a hug.

Her chest was heaving with deep breaths as
she tried to control herself. A mix of sobbing rage
was building pressure inside her like a mountain
barely containing its lava. She couldn't find her
voice; the wind had been sucked from her lungs.
The sword trembled in the air, pointed at his
throat.

He didn't seem to care. His eyes finally
lingered on her face. The deep scars gnarled his
eye and made it impossible for him to fully open
the right one. The skin was riddled with white
and black streaks, the ink from his tattoo smeared
slowly as the burns healed. She said nothing,
trying to control the frantic emotions crawling up
her throat, crawling up her tongue, curling in her
mouth. The terrible screams. The rage, the fear,
the anger, the hate, and the sorrow, the nonstop
terrible sorrow of the loss of her only child. The
only child she would ever carry, the only child she
would ever hold, stolen before its first suckle.
Ripped from her before she had even changed her
diaper. *Lucille*. She couldn't say it again. But her
brain screamed it, echoing across the room in

earth-shattering pain.

When she had first gone to prison, the pain was so strong and so powerful it amazed her that the walls could still stand. Surely they would wilt and crumble like her soul. When she clawed her skin so raw and bloody that they handcuffed her to a bed and sedated her, she wondered how the earth itself hadn't exploded. How could it hold together against such pain? The universe could surely crack from the force of it. It was so large, it was so strong.

But somehow, the planet withstood all that pain and agony. Somehow, the walls still stood. Even the cuffs held. And the pain oozing out her skin in little drops of red learned to sit dormant inside her like a silent disease. She taught it to sit in the corner and say nothing. But here it was, rearing its ugly head. Here it came bursting through her skin, setting fire to her lungs, scorching her vocal cords, and screaming, screaming within her. It couldn't sit in the corner again. *Lucille*.

He lunged at her, grabbing her wrist and pulling her close, and he wrapped his arms around her tightly from behind. His erection was pressed against her ass and she did nothing. She trembled harder, her whole body revolting inside her. Her limbs betrayed her, just as her voice betrayed her. Her empty left hand was already scratching and tearing away bits of her flesh. His embrace was warm, and for a tiny breath, she almost relaxed. His mouth was pressed tightly to her ear, and she felt his tiny kisses.

He ran his tongue across the top of her ear and he said the words that brought life back to her body-that called her brain back from the lost place- he said the thing that shoved that painful rage-filled grief back into the corner. The very words he said snapped her back into game mode.

"Let's go get her."

A cry gurgled out of Jaspierre's throat, and her knees grew weak, and he held her tightly. She kissed him. Right on his gnarled, burned lips. "Lucille is alive?" she uttered in hoarse, raspy tears. He nodded and they kissed again. The whole room spun with ecstasy. Her brain returned, and her vision un-blurred, and she saw she was kissing Chance. She was kissing the man that stole her only daughter. The monster. She stepped back and stared at him. "Did you touch her?" The blade rose to his throat, not even the slightest tremor this time.

He raised his hands innocently. "Never. I didn't fuck her, or fuck her up. I never even slapped her." He paused, glancing at the blade, then back at Jaspierre. "I don't have a death wish."

JASPIERRE'S LAST CHANCE

"You gave her away!" Jaspierre shouted, charging at him. The blade slipped into the meat of his left arm as he tried to block.

"I had to! You were in prison, you bitch! If I had kept her, you *know* what would have happened." He charged back at her, slamming her into the wall behind her. "You *know*! You already *know*!" He kissed her again as her body squirmed between him and the solid wall. "I love you, Jaspierre. I'd do anything for you. I would *never* risk her." In a surge of emotion, he kissed her neck again. She wasn't fighting back.

Her lips hovered close to his ear. "Where is my daughter?"

His hands slid up her arms, holding them over her head, pressed against the wall. He was panting into her mouth, desperately wanting to kiss her, to fuck her, to kill her.

"Let's go get our baby." He nibbled on her neck, his body demanding hers.

Arnold opened the front door, two servals pulling hard on the leash. It was the teen and Ikali. Chance and Jaspierre pulled apart, somehow both of them embarrassed. Her mind was spinning. What the fuck was she doing?

Chapter

Seventeen

Edward was sitting in his worn recliner, watching the news casually when he saw the report of stolen servals at the zoo. He got so flustered with excitement he could barely pay attention, entirely missing the few sentences on the deaths of the zookeepers. He couldn't help but grin when he imagined her walking out of the zoo with her cats on leashes.

She'd probably end up back in prison. But damn, she just walked in and took them. He tried to hide his grin with his hand. *This is the wrong reaction*, he thought. But he ended up giggling. *She was so cool.* He picked up the phone to call her, but he imagined she wouldn't pick up. She had her hands full of those servals. But wouldn't it be awesome if she could march in and get Lucille back like that?

Was he supposed to charge down there and make her give them back? He wasn't sure she'd ever be willing to do that. But he got in his car anyway. An hour or so later, he was standing on her marble steps, still grinning like a fool. Who just walks in and takes a whole pen of wild animals from a zoo? Sure, her servals were probably moderately well behaved, but were the others? *Sheesh, Jaspierre, what is wrong with you?*

The heat of laughter burned his cheeks. He took a deep breath and tried to calm down. He had to be stern so he could coax her to return the wild cats she had stolen. He let out his last giggling laugh and knocked on the door, trying to rein in his merriment. She was the most impossible creature he had ever met. Gorgeous, rich, wild, and daring. She was dangerous and perfect. He used to feel like everything was so black and white. People were good or bad with very little room for in between. But she wasn't a monster. She was a survivor and a fighter and just breathtakingly delicious.

He knocked again, trying to harden himself against her beautiful eyes. "Give them back, you silly girl." That was what he'd say.

The door creaked open and a tall, thin man with grey hair stood nervously. His eye was swollen shut. He was flicking his fingers to his thumb, back and forth in a frantic pace. His lips were moving, but he wasn't making any sounds. "Where is Jaspierre?" Edward said, concerned that there seemed to be a new man in the house.

Arnold's nervous tic froze for a moment, and he stared into Edward's eyes. "Chance." He flicked his fingers again quickly and Edward suddenly realized this man's arm was dislocated.

"He took her. Canada, I think." Then Arnold whimpered, "One-two-three-four-four-three-two-one. You should hurry: he's gonna kill her."

* * * * * * * * * * * *

Three hours later, she was in the car with Chance. They were driving back to Canada. He wasn't taking the most direct routes, and she wasn't sure if that was to extend their hours in the car together or if that was to avoid something specific on the highway.

"Do you remember when we were kids, and we found that knife? Sheesh, we had to have been five or six."

"I remember."

26 YEARS EARLIER

Chance pressed his lips together again and tried to whistle. Spit flew from his lips and onto Jaspierre's face. "Ew stop! You gotta blow gentler."

He blew again, softer, and said, "I don't think I'm ever gonna learn."

"You will. Practice makes perfect. Mother's been teaching me to stitch straight stitches. She says if I keep at it, I'll be able to do them quickly and correctly," Jaspierre lied. She spent many hours lying about what went on with her and Mother. Even at five years of age, she knew to keep secrets. She had, in fact, been practicing stitches, and Mother did say she should keep at it, sort of. Mother beat her and said *try again*, over and over, until finally she had a straight line done in ten minutes. Mother said people would still die from her shitty stitches, but at least they'd die slower.

They had been practicing on a bit of leather, but the idea of stabbing a person over and over with a needle made her stomach flip.

Jaspierre learned to excel at eliminating the details that made people uncomfortable. Even though everyone killed, or stitched people in the basement or whatever, it wasn't exactly kosher to talk about it. Those were private things.

"Do you wanna go walk in the field by the barn? I think I saw some frogs out there," Jaspierre said.

"Toads. Frogs live in water, toads live in fields. I read a book about 'em," Chance replied.

"Fine, a toad then." They skipped together down the brick path and the three brick steps. The path turned to the right, to the barn, but they stepped off it and ran left. Jaspierre stopped at a small oak tree. It was just barely big enough to climb. "I think he lives near this tree."

They started searching, never very far from each other, Chance still spitting as he discreetly tried to learn to whistle. Just as Chance shouted that he found a big ol' toad, Jaspierre saw the sparkling glint of something metal.

She curiously walked closer, sliding down a sharp hill. At the bottom of the little hill was a thin stream of water. She wondered if that was what she saw sparkling, but she thought for sure it had been a piece of metal. She turned to climb back up the hill, when she saw him. He was a thin man, he wasn't moving, and his eyes were wide open.

A bright shiny blade stuck out of his belly into the sun. It sparkled hard into her eyes, and she shifted position so she could look at it. The handle was gold, with a smooth spot right in the middle. Carved deeply into the smooth golden color was the letter J.

Jaspierre was mesmerized. Completely ignoring the man, she leaned forward to examine the handle more carefully.

There was a hand guard to prevent the hand from sliding forward into the blade. The blade was very thin, long, and very slightly curved. It was absolutely beautiful. Hadn't she read a book about this sort of thing? The sword in the stone! Only the true hero could pull it.

It had her letter on it, carved perfectly in a fancy script on the handle of that blade. Was this hers?

She glanced around. There wasn't anyone else here. In fact, Chance seemed to be just out of earshot. On the steep incline, she reached out as far as she could. She did not want to step on the man when she carefully pulled the blade. Her fingertips strained, and the metal felt cold against her touch. It rumbled slightly, it seemed. Her fingertip held it and she closed her eyes. It wasn't rumbling. It was thumping. *Thump, thump. Thump, thump.*

She opened her eyes and turned her head, certain it was Chance's big footsteps crashing down the hill, but she didn't see him. Her fingertips gently rolled around the blade and she grasped it again. She closed her eyes, straining her ears. What was it? *Thump thump. Thump thump.*

There was a raspy whoosh of air, and Jaspierre turned and shouted, "Chance! I know you are here. Come out and see what I found."

But he didn't step from behind a bush or a tree. He didn't shout *Geronimo!* like he sometimes did. The little wooded area was quiet. She turned back and looked at the sword. This time, her finger gently traced the perfect carving of her letter J.

A tickle on her leg made her mindlessly reach down to scratch it while she stared at the letter. But her hand bumped something. A bug, or snake or something. Something bad. And she screamed and leapt backwards. Fingers were grasping at her pant leg.

Fingers connected to a hand, connected to the arm of the man, who was staring at her with big eyes. He gasped a loud whistling airy sound and his mouth opened and closed like a doll without a voice box. His mouth moved up and down. He was talking, he was trying to talk, but he couldn't. Not with that sword in him, holding down his body. It was stopping him from talking.

Crashing down the hill in a sliding, smashing motion, Chance was suddenly by her side. "I heard you scream! What happened?" His eyes grew wide with fright as he saw the man with the wild terrified eyes wheezing on the ground. His mouth was moving up and down, but nothing more than air came out of his throat.

"He can't talk because of the sword." Jaspierre said, matter-of-fact. "I think it's pinning his voice down."

"Okay." Chance nodded. "Do you think we should pull it out and then he can tell us why your Mother did this to him? Or do you think we should leave him?"

She held his hand and they looked at each other. Mother did not like it when children interfered. Jaspierre looked back at the man, with his frantic, terrified eyes. "If you pull it, do you think you could stab it back in if you have to? If he says it was Mother, you're right, we should leave him."

"I'm sure I can. He's barely able to move."

And with that load of shit in his head, his little six-year-old hand pulled on the blade stuck in the man the same way a butterfly is pinned to a frame.

He convulsed immediately, spurting out blood from his chest in a little bubbling geyser. Jaspierre covered her eyes. Chance watched, mouth open, reaching forward to touch the little red gurgles. His hand came back coated in red slime. "Well, that didn't work," he said with a calm disinterest in human suffering.

Jaspierre had a sudden welling up of tears. "I wish I could have stitched him. Maybe if I was quicker."

"Do you think we need to hide him now?"

"Why?" she asked.

"Because we killed him, and that's a crime, so we gotta hide him so we don't go to prison," Chance said very calmly. "We'll need shovels and stuff."

"Are you sure? I've never seen Mother hide any dead people before. Are you sure it's a crime?"

"Of course I'm sure. I'm gonna be a cop, so I need to know the rules."

Jaspierre rolled this around in her head. What *did* Mother do with bodies? She'd have to ask. "I want that sword; it's mine. It's got my letter on it."

JASPIERRE'S LAST CHANCE

Chance rubbed the sword carefully on the dead man's pants. "That's as clean as I can get it. It's a pretty cool sword." He carefully handed it to her. It was longer than her leg, and she could barely carry it without it dragging on the ground behind her. They walked away from the dead man and Chance rinsed off his red hand in the tiny stream of water. She said, "Stand back. I'm gonna swing it."

Chance stepped backwards and she spun in a circle, twirling her skirt open and the blade smacked into a tree, catching it hard. Jaspierre grabbed her arm. "Ouch! That hurt." She shook her hand, the blade still sitting in the tree. When she put her hand back on, she couldn't pull it loose. "Hey, I can't get it. Will you help me, Chance?"

He wrapped his arms around her and they both pulled hard. The blade suddenly popped loose and immediately sliced into Chance's bicep. Tears welled up in his eyes and they poured over. Jaspierre checked his gaping wound and said, "This is bad. We're going to have to show Mother."

CHAPTER

EIGHTEEN

"Do you remember Mother being married?" Jaspierre asked Chance. He was sitting in the driver's seat with thick black sunglasses. He had a grin still plastered on his face, even though it had been hours.

They had been riding silently, Jaspierre still too overwhelmed to make conversation. Not only was Lucille alive, but she hadn't been destroyed by Chance. This seemed remarkable, and shone Chance in a new light in her eyes. Yes, he was bad. But deep down, wasn't everyone?

She wondered briefly if Arnold would feed Dru and the other miscreants in the basement. It didn't really matter to her much either way, but it would be awfully nice if Dru survived long enough to answer her next round of questions.

Chance glanced at her briefly, grinned

again, and then his eyes lingered on the road. "Are you saying you don't remember if she was married?"

Jaspierre sighed with irritation. They felt like kids again, friendly, annoyed banter already falling into its old rhythms."If I remembered, would I ask you about it?"

Chance smirked and stared at road kill they were driving up to. It was a raccoon, and its body was inflated and large. Chance thwacked over the top of it and the squishy pop of its body could be felt throughout the car. A hot smell of decomposing flesh abruptly rushed into the air. Jaspierre cringed.

"God, why did you have to do that?" she grumbled and crossed her arms, trying not to breathe.

Completely ignoring her, he was all smiles and cotton candy. "I just can't believe you'd forget. It seems like he was around a lot. Dru. Don't you remember him?"

She shook her head. Her lungs burned with the effort to keep them from doing their job. *Wait just a few more seconds and maybe that awful rotting coon will have whooshed right on by.*

"Well, actually, I guess he left when we were pretty young." Chance seemed completely unaffected by the rancid stench. "Remember

Liddy? Yeah, well, she hadn't even..." He paused but then laughed. "I almost said left, but that seems ridiculous. I might as well say 'died.'" He shook his head, grinning. "Died. She hadn't even died, and Dru had already come and gone. Maybe you don't remember him because you always tried to avoid him. Don't you remember?"

"I don't remember him at all." In fact, all Jaspierre could remember was that he was familiar. That wasn't particularly notable, though. Many people seemed familiar, or were familiar. Jaspierre didn't have time to worry about those kinds of details. "What do you remember about him?"

"I remember being mad at him." Chance didn't say why, but Jaspierre guessed it had something to do with Liddy. She was wrong, though. It had something to do with her. Everything about Chance always came back to her. Liddy's inevitable murder, Dru's leaving; it was all about Jaspierre, as everything would always be.

"Do you think Mother loved him?" Jaspierre trembled a little. Wouldn't it be just awful if Mother did love someone? A man, instead of her own flesh and blood?

"Your mother? God no. I don't think she loved anything."

JASPIERRE'S LAST CHANCE

And there it was. Jaspierre had a sharp ping of annoyance. Why did he have to say it like that? Jaspierre let out a frustrated sigh. "How could she have been married?" It wasn't a question, but more like a depressed resolution. She'd never understand Mother, and she'd never get to ask her questions to figure her out. She'd never make her proud. Mother was the most unsatisfying person, and yet, one of the few people that consumed Jaspierre's thoughts.

What would Mother think of her now? Still incapable of murdering the one man who deserved it more than anyone. Worse than simply unsuccessful slaughter, she was riding with him. Hell, she had kissed him, but Mother wouldn't have given a rat's ass about that. Kissing was just another weapon in the tool belt. Jaspierre hadn't kissed him to hurt him, though.

She kissed him because he let Lucille live. He kept her safe and let her live. She wouldn't have even thought it was possible for Chance to do such a thing. He struggled with carnal desires more than anyone else she knew. The desire to maim, kill, fuck, and who the hell knew what else he'd been up to. But somehow, he protected the tiny blond curly-haired baby.

It was a miracle.

"How long until we see her?"

JASPIERRE'S LAST CHANCE

"Shit, it's a long fucking drive. Tomorrow." Jaspierre wondered if she would have to fuck him or if he would give her back Lucille before he expected so much from her. But, once Lucille was hers, Chance would go back to being the first person on her list to eliminate.

Until then, when in Rome.

They stopped at a ratty old gas station. There was a lean, grey-haired man at the counter. Chance grabbed a bag of chips and an energy drink. The man stared nervously at Chance's scarred, tattooed face. He looked like he had been mauled. The dark tattooed shadows in the grooves of his gnarled flesh made them more prominent than ever.

Jaspierre wondered if the skinny old man was reaching for his gun. He was certainly shifting back and forth from foot to foot in a nervous way. "You want anything?" Chance said, and suddenly was standing close. He was standing fucking close. *"Fuck me" close.*

His warm hand pressed on the middle of her back, and her skin started to crawl. It was screaming to run, *run the fuck away from Chance--he's going to hurt you.* Jaspierre knew he would. Hell, Chance knew he would too. But they couldn't stop themselves. She needed Lucille. Chance wanted Jaspierre. They were both moments away from the thing they wanted more than life itself. So if he hurt her, so be it.

And they both knew it.

CHAPTER

NINETEEN

Edward found himself frantically driving down the road. What the hell was his plan? He was on the main highway, flying towards Canada as though he could find her, as though he *would* find her. What the fuck was his plan!

How long ago was her head start? *Fuck.* She was gonna get killed, he just knew it. He should have been staying with her. They knew, they both fucking knew that Chance was going to show up. He should have stayed with her!

His blood was swishing around his body like an overloaded washing machine. There was no focus left, the yellow dotted lines flying past the cop's car far faster than they should. Too fast.

He turned the radio dial until he synced with the cops in this area. He was too far behind; he'd never catch them. He didn't even know where they were going!

The radio cackled with news of a gas station attendant shot by a man and a woman. Edward pulled over and quickly looked up the location. They were going the same direction as he was, but they were on the side roads, the quiet ones. At least an hour or more ahead of him. He pulled back on the main highway. Chance couldn't keep his fucking gun put away and he would leave a trail of bodies to follow. Where the fuck could they be going? If Jaspierre helped kill the man at the gas station, then why the fuck was she helping him?

Lucille.

26 YEARS EARLIER

The walk home seemed extraordinarily long, with Chance sniffling and holding his bleeding arm, and Jaspierre trying to drag the long blade behind her. It rattled on the rocks as she walked. If Jaspierre thought she could, she would have stitched Chance up herself, but she didn't want him to die. Mother said she was too slow and people would die.

She couldn't risk killing Chance from her crappy inability to stitch. That would be terrible. It was one thing to leave a dead man in the woods, it was completely different to kill your only friend. They finally made it to the brick path near the barn and stepped up the three brick steps. As they walked down the path, the sword rattled on the bricks behind her. It was a glorious sound, like one she'd never heard before. Sharp, deadly metal rattling against blood red bricks. When they stepped inside, Liddy was making lunch in the kitchen.

Liddy was Chance's aunt, and she seemed to have her hands full with him most of the time. "Hey, Liddy, where is Mother?"

"Severina is in her office. I don't know if she'll want to be disturbed by you two." Liddy didn't comment on the large bloodstain growing on Chance's sleeve. Ignoring the problem was Liddy's special talent. She could seemingly ignore anything and everything. She ignored it when Mother hit her, or worse, when Mother hit Jaspierre. She ignored it when Chance bled or cried. It was like she lived inside her head.

"Why are you making lunch? Where's Chef?" Jaspierre asked, staring at the bologna sandwiches.

"He had a family emergency, so you're stuck with me today. I'm sure Severina won't be particularly pleased, but ah well, it can't be helped. He's not here." Liddy continued to fiddle with the plates, clearly nervous about bringing such plain fare to the lady of the house. Liddy didn't know how to make much besides boxed mac and cheese and sandwiches. She loitered in the kitchen. "Go on and tell her you are back."

Even Jaspierre understood Liddy wanted

her to say hello to Mother first. Perhaps while Mother slugged her in the stomach, Liddy could just set the plated sandwich and run. Jaspierre and Chance were going to be the distraction, even the bait. Jaspierre knew this, but she wasn't afraid of Mother.

That was a lie; Mother was terrifying to everyone. But Jaspierre knew the worst it could get was a beating, and she could handle it. She rapped loudly on the door, and her knuckles cried in sharp pain as she cracked them across the wood. She didn't allow herself to wince. If Mother saw her cringing, that'd be the end of this adventure to get stitches. Besides, she had a question for Mother.

What did she do with the bodies?

Severina opened the door casually. She was in a floor-length black dress with a sheer slit that curled around her body like smoke from a cigarette. "Chance needs stitches. Would you mind helping him out?" Jaspierre stood as tall as she dared, holding her shoulders proudly in a perfect line. Mother would never tolerate a little girl who slouched.

"Please, ma'am. If it's not too much trouble. Liddy ain't gonna take me in." He held out his arm, and the wound was deep and bloody.

Severina stared curiously at it, then turned

back to her only child. "What have we here?"

"I found this in a man out by that tiny little stream of water. Chance plucked it out, and I'd like to keep it. See here? It's got my letter on it." Jaspierre proudly held up the blade. The tip was ragged and dulled by its long trek against the bricks. Severina looked at it for a moment, and then turned and grabbed a little mending kit from her desk drawer.

"I will mend him." Jaspierre figured Mother liked to do stitches. Mother liked to do a great many things that most people would cringe at. Once, a few weeks ago, Jaspierre watched Mother carefully take a chunk of skin off a man's leg. He had been sitting in the living room and said something awful. Jaspierre couldn't, for the life of her, remember what it was he said. But she remembered Mother jumping up and shouting before she shoved the chloroform rag into the man's mouth. Jaspierre had run to her room and hid in her closet. It was best to be away when Mother was like this. But Mother told her later that peeling off that bit of skin was like ripping loose bark off a tree; not a big deal at all.

Jaspierre watched as the dark blue thread slid through the tiny opening in the needle. Severina grabbed Chance's arm and shoved the needle in. No chloroform. Jaspierre wasn't even sure she had sterilized the wound. Chance gasped loudly, and tears trickled down both cheeks, but he didn't move. His mouth clenched into a tight white line, and the color drained from his face. She stitched him quickly, and in less than five minutes, he was done.

"There now, go find out what's for lunch." The boy turned and promptly fainted. He could handle holding still and resisting the pain, but he couldn't get the blood flow back to his head.

Jaspierre stared at her collapsed friend on the floor. "Mother, did you stitch him too slowly?" A hot slap burned across her cheek. Jaspierre winced, but turned to Mother and timidly asked, "Is he dead or not?"

"He fainted, you fucking idiot. You'll never be smart like me if you don't learn to use your brain! What is wrong with you!" Severina scolded her, finger pointing in her face.

Jaspierre held back a worried sob. Now or never. "Mother, I want to ask you something before you go back to work. Is that okay?" The right side of her face still burned from the slap, and the red handprint welted up.

Severina simply stared, not bothering to answer. Jaspierre was on her own. If she asked and Mother didn't approve, another slap or a one-two punch in the kisser. Or stomach. Jaspierre braced her stomach as much as she could. "What do you do with the bodies? Is it a crime to kill them? Are you going to go to jail?" As terrifying as Mother was, being alone scared Jaspierre more. What would happen to her if Mother was gone?

Severina let out a bright, beautiful, and genuine laugh. Jaspierre had only heard her truly laugh a few times. "It's only a little bit illegal. It's like shoplifting a candy bar, or speeding down a road. Everyone does it. You only do the time if you get caught. Why would I get caught? I'm too smart for that, and you are too. Besides, if they ever even got a scent on me, I'd set them sniffing on someone else. As far as the bodies go, haven't you been paying attention? They get disposed, or burned, or shredded, or used as parts. There are no leftovers. I'll show you how to burn a body tomorrow, then you'll see. Then you'll know."

"Thank you, Mother." Jaspierre bent down and grabbed Chance's hands and slowly dragged him out of the room. Liddy stood on the other side of the doorway with a plate in her hands.

"Is she in a good mood today?" Liddy said, ignoring her unconscious nephew. He was already starting to stir a little anyway.

"I think maybe. She wants her lunch," Jaspierre whispered back.

The door swung shut behind Liddy, and a

moment later, a loud slapping sound. Mother must have been in a good mood.

JASPIERRE'S LAST CHANCE

CHAPTER

TWENTY

Chance's nose found itself running up her neck, sniffing her intensely. He was already panting with the effort to hold back. He'd love to fuck her and kill her now. His teeth dug into his tongue and he stepped away from her. *He did not want to kill her!*

He stepped tightly against the counter, refusing to let his eyes linger in her direction. Her smell was intense and perfect. *Do not kill her.* Just fuck her. *Fuck her and fuck her and fuck her.*

Control was not a skill he had mastered. He raised the gun in his right hand, pointing it at the skinny grey-haired man. She placed her hand on his arm. He turned and looked at her. Her eyes were clear as a bell. She could control herself whenever she wanted. His fingers twitched to turn the gun toward her. Would her face be as pretty splattered on the floor? Somehow, he thought it would be even better than ever.

But then it would be over, and he desperately wanted her to linger. His lips sucked at hers and right as he slipped his tongue into her mouth, the bullet leapt from the gun and exploded the skull of the thin, grey man.

Chance was so aroused he started tearing her grey dress up, frantic for release with his empty left hand. The right hand still held the gun. She was calm and did nothing. Both of her hands slowly started to raise into the air. He couldn't get her pants unbuttoned with just his left hand and started to use his teeth. His right hand still held the gun. She was so calm. He stopped and glanced up at her, and then he realized he was holding the gun at her face. *Shit*.

"Sorry, old habits." He lowered the gun and fumbled at her pants again, but it was too late. Angry crawled over his arousal. She didn't want him. Here he thought she was into it, but he was waving that fucking gun at her face. How the fuck could he have messed that up so much?

She hadn't moved. Jaspierre's hands were still in the air. She looked calm but unhappy. Hell if he was going to fuck her while she was unhappy. Not like this.

He grabbed his energy drink and a bag of

chips. "Get your shit. Let's go." Jaspierre seemed frozen in time, still unwavering. He turned and his fury grew. Why couldn't she just be eager to screw like a normal woman? What had fucked her up so much to make her such a close-legged nun?

His feet grew heavy as he stomped towards the door. She didn't move.

He looked back at her, and she had a wild, dreamy look on her face. His heart was pounding harder. Like she wasn't even there. Anger was building inside him. *Her hands were still in the air.*

Everything in his hands crashed to the ground as he charged at her. She crumpled into a shelf of chips and the two of them and the shelf crashed to the ground. His teeth clenched into her neck and she let out a cry. He could feel her muscles moving in his mouth, writhing in his teeth. Salty blood burst into his mouth. She squirmed underneath him, her body making full contact with his.

He released her neck with his teeth and held his face over hers. He saw little drops of blood dripping from his teeth onto her face. *Do not kill her!* His body was trembling with desire. Her eyes suddenly snapped tightly to his. For the barest breath of a second, he grew afraid. Deep inside him flashed a warning. *Stop or die.*

He paid it no mind and licked her cheek,

pausing to pant, his lips a hair from hers. She
smiled.

26 YEARS EARLIER

Jaspierre rattled the little sword behind her as she walked up the stairs. She rattled it across the floor while she walked to the little playroom. It was a delicious sound. Scratchity scratch. Vibrations rumbling up her fingertips. Mother said that this year, she'd go to kindergarten. She wasn't sure what kindergarten would be like, but probably wouldn't be worse than those board meetings Mother dragged her to.

She set up a few pillows and swung the long blade into them. It bounced off. She could barely get it moving without twirling her entire body. She wondered, half-heartedly, if someone could teach her to use it. Chance refused to play swords with her, declaring it unsafe, and he didn't want more stitches. The stitches had grown infected, despite his and Jaspierre's efforts to clean the wound daily. Eventually, he got so sick that he had to stay in bed. Today, Jaspierre was alone with her blade, Chance was lying half-dead in his bed, and she was trying to dice a pillow.

She rattled the blade behind her on the floor. It tickled her insides somehow. She could feel the tiny clatter all the way up into her shoulder. It made her teeth feel like they could sing almost. Maybe the sword wasn't sharp anymore. She looked at the edge and it was pitted and worn. The tip was dented and dinged. She couldn't cut a pillow with it like this. Probably it couldn't even cut a piece of paper.

She let it clack across the floor as she wandered to the kitchen. Chef was there. They had many chefs; some were tall or fat or thin, but Jaspierre learned that they were just called Chef. Mother did not like it if you used their regular names. She said something about separation of Church and State. Jaspierre didn't really know what that meant. But she did know what Mother meant.

Chef--whichever one he was--could not be trusted. Chef was not someone to tell secrets to, or to talk about private matters. Like murders or corpse burning. Mother had certainly taught Jaspierre a lesson about roasting a human. She didn't know who he was, just that he smelled terrible when he burned. Jaspierre had to haul a lot of wood to burn that body for Mother. Mother made her stay up all night, sleeping in half hour increments, before rousing her with a slap to put more wood on. Staying out of prison was not a task for the weak or the lazy.

It took preparations and a lot of wood. A lot of wood.

Chef couldn't be trusted with those private matters. Jaspierre thought that Severina's normal hiring site, Viscardine, was not a good place to hire chefs because anyone they hired from there could talk about private matters. The maids, Liddy, or the gardeners, or the barn helpers. They would see a body, clean it up, and all day long, they'd have good luck. That was what Mother said.

Perhaps it was true and lucky. Jaspierre hadn't felt particularly lucky the day the body had been fully seared in the fireplace. She hoped that perhaps she'd find something marvelous outside. Like a baby toad--all day long, she was supposed to be lucky! But despite her mother's promises, she hadn't been lucky at all.

Until dinnertime. Chef had made her the most marvelous apple pie. Jaspierre loved apples. So perhaps Mother was right, and cleaning up corpses did make her lucky. This Chef seemed particularly nice, and maybe he would know about swords.

"Can you show me how to make this sharper?" Jaspierre spun in a circle so she could get the blade up on the counter. She missed, and it bounced against the edge of the counter, knocking her backwards. "Sorry, it's heavy."

Chef stared at the little girl. "Does Severina..." He paused for a long time. "Okay. I can show you how to sharpen that sword."

He carefully showed Jaspierre how to sharpen the sword with his knife block. "You carefully slide it down the blade, and all these little nicks smooth right out. Look, you'll have to be very careful. It's going to be very sharp when we are done. It's not a toy. It's a blade. Treat it with respect."

Jaspierre lay on the floor next to the long blade and slowly slid the block from one end to the other. "Do you know of anyone who can teach me to swing it? I want to learn."

Chef was busy chopping carrots. His knife went *thump thump thump* hard and fast.

"Hey, do you know or not?" she said again, shouting over his knife skills. Liddy walked into the kitchen with her broom.

"What have you done!" she shouted at Chef. "What have you done!"

He looked up, concern sliding across his face. "What?" His face grew flushed red.

"Did you do this to the floors? Are you trying to make her kill me? Look at these scratches! Look at them!" Her voice grew higher and higher pitched, more and more frantic.

Chef looked puzzled and turned to see what she meant. As he turned, somehow, he stepped on Jaspierre's little foot. He yelped and jumped backwards, trying to avoid falling on the child, and he slipped; no, he slid. He slid face first, hands down, over Jaspierre and onto the blade. It pierced right through him, the knife sticking out his back unexpectedly quick. Liddy let out a shout. "She's going to kill me!" Liddy frantically left the kitchen. Back to scrubbing at the floors on her hands and knees. Liddy was perfectly inside herself- ignoring.

Jaspierre watched Chef as his face twitched and flickered and he gagged hard, shaking all over before he quit. A deep sadness sank into her belly, followed by a rush of guilt. Immediately, she was overcome with anger. "How dare you die! How dare you? Why would you do that to me! You make apple pies!" Her throat grew raw from the angry cries of terror. Her body trembled. He slowly died on top of her. It took all her effort to push him off of her. She took his arms and

helplessly tried to tug him to the fireplace.
"Where's my good luck now? Where is it now?
How could you do this to me!"

Find a body, clean it up, all day long...

Chapter

Twenty-One

Chance's bloody face was too fucking close to hers. It seemed like she lost herself for a moment and now she was crumpled in a pile of shelves and chips with a horny as fuck monster humping on her legs. He was holding back, and she liked that. She didn't have any reason to hold back.

Lucille.

Well, okay, one reason. But that didn't mean she was going to fuck him or be fucked by him. Well, actually, maybe she would, because she was gonna get her baby back and she didn't give a shit what she had to do.

But she wasn't going to do it unless it was the absolutely last option.

And then she smiled.

Her left arm had been pinned underneath

her when she fell. But her right arm was positioned just perfectly. She gently wrapped it around his most prized possession. He let out a happy sound. She pressed her lips into his ear. "I will rip this off your body."

He shuddered. His every tremble crawled through her like a tapeworm. He started to grind into her hand and she squeezed so hard, he let out a scream. "I will fucking rip this off your body." Her tone grew low and intense.

He finally got the message and froze. Almost certainly he was debating whether he should snap her like a twig or let her up. "Chance," she said with a soft, warm tone. "I want Lucille."

"You owe me!" he shrieked.

"You. Owe. Me!" she said back in a loud growl, clenching her hand tight. Tears formed on his eyes. She twisted and crushed with all her might. "You fucking owe me!"

He let out a scream and punched the shelf next to her face repeatedly. As soon as she released him, he leapt backwards, doubled over. "You fucking bitch."

She grabbed a new set of energy drinks and an armful of chips. "Ready yet or do you want ice for your balls?"

"Fucking bitch." He hobbled to the truck

and climbed in, cursing repeatedly. They sat for a few minutes, her furious and silent, him shouting and punching the steering wheel before Chance finally started the truck. "We'll see her in a few more hours, and you better be fucking grateful."

Jaspierre nodded and they pulled out of the gas station.

A red car pulled in to the pump, and Jaspierre heard their door shut. She wondered if there would be a cop on their tails soon. "Well, if you don't want to talk about Dru, you wanna tell me what you've been up to while I was rotting away in there?" She didn't turn her head to look at him, still staring out the passenger window. He was silent. A few minutes later, Jaspierre heard the first squeals of a siren.

Chance didn't seem to notice. He was clenching his teeth, his fingers wrapped tightly around the steering wheel. When she looked over, she found herself staring at his gnarled, scarred face. Chance never particularly struck her as handsome, but now he was downright gruesome looking. Burning him alive might not have killed him, but it took its toll. The skin had wrinkled into stiff patterns, hills, and valleys like strings had been snaked in and out of his flesh. He had tattooed these peaks and valleys in black and white colors so they were impossible to avoid looking at.

"I built us a house, you know? I built it real nice in the woods. Just for you, Jaspierre, then you had to go get caught up with the cops." The heat of his anger was strong. "Right before I got these tattoos. I didn't even get to show you the best one." He pulled his shirt down with his left hand. She could see the part that said "pier" in red slit lines.

"That looks very realistic," she said. She didn't have to see the rest. She knew. It looked like he had razored her name into his chest moments earlier and they were just about to drip with blood. It was a fucking realistic tattoo.

"Dammit. Why do you have to be so fucking awful?" He wasn't asking a question, shifting in his seat because his balls still ached steadily. "I went to Canada. That's where I put her; there are a man and a woman taking care of her. They are legit too. Really wanted a baby, no drugs or that fucked up shit. I visit when I'm..." He almost said "between corpses." "Between clients." That sounded like he was some sort of man prostitute, and he snorted back a laugh. "I've just been doing my thing."

Jaspierre ran her fingers through her long hair. It would have been nice if she had a few wigs for this race across the country. She didn't exactly want to be recognized too easily. There were two ways to hide. One was to stand out, like bright blue hair; that was memorable. Having a memorable, *removable* thing prevented people from remembering anything else. All they remembered was blue. The other way was to be such a shadow on the wall they could barely remember you were even in the room.

Two ways.

Neither were working. Chance wasn't about to be a shadow. And it was not like he could remove his head and thus his tattoos. She suddenly snickered. Removing his head wasn't entirely off the table.

"I'm not the monster you think I am," Chance said. "I kept our daughter safe. I came to get you and bring you home. I wish you could just see that."

Jaspierre's eyes wandered to the landscape. "I am glad you kept her safe." But inside, her stomach flipped. What did he mean "bring you home"? Where were they going?

JASPIERRE'S LAST CHANCE

CHAPTER

TWENTY-TWO

They drove up to a gated community. Jaspierre looked at the white iron gate, then through it to the perfect houses. They were large and beautiful. Which house was Lucille in? Was it the yellow one on the corner? Did she live in the blue house at the end of the cul-de-sac? Where did she go to school? Did she have friends?

Chance pointed to the yellow house on the corner. "There." Jaspierre stared. The house reminded her of a small version of her own house. White columns, five large steps up to the glamorous front door. In the top right window, a pink curtain fluttered. That had to be her room!

"What are you waiting for? Let's go in." Jaspierre was almost out of her seat, pressing her face out the window, straining her eyes for more details. Was her little girl in that bedroom?

"I don't have the code."

Jaspierre pulled her head back in the car. "What?"

"I don't have the code to open the gate."

Jaspierre's eyes grew wide. "You told me, you fucking told me you took care of her!" She lunged at him in the car, blind rage rippling up her throat, out her mouth. "You fucking told me!" Her hands clawed desperately at him, but his hands locked on her wrists. She was strong enough to get one hard smack on his face. She leaned in close. "You fucking liar."

He kissed her nose while she panted furiously, and she tried to hit him again. "Let's go break our baby out, okay?"

"You fucking shit head," she replied, but stopped fighting him. He smiled, and she wrinkled her nose and continued, "How do we get her?"

"I don't know."

She stared at the gate. She wouldn't be able to walk around it, and although there wasn't a guard, there was a code box at the front. Chance had parked a bit to the side of the gate, where they could look in. A car drove up and the driver punched in a code and slipped through. The gate moved very quickly. They definitely couldn't follow a car in.

"Let's see if we can get it open." They drove up to the box and it had the numbers 0-9 listed on it. Jaspierre wasn't even sure how many digits the other car pressed. Chance pressed the numbers 1425 and pressed call. There was a loud buzzing sound, but then silence. He tried again.

1467

Buzz.

Nothing.

1435

Buzz.

Nothing.

1446

Buzz.

"What are you doing?" Jaspierre said, and right then, she heard a feeble "Hello."

"Hello, ma'am." It was his cop voice. Jaspierre grinned. His deep, reassuring voice he used on people while they were at a traffic stop. Chance continued, "Ma'am, I am here to deliver a pizza, and I'd really love it if you could buzz me in. I tried buzzing to the Jacka's house, they're the yellow one on the corner, and they didn't answer, but their pie is gettin' awful cold."

There was no reply, just another buzz. The gate swung open, and Chance quickly zoomed inside. He did not park in front of the yellow house, instead sliding up the driveway at the blue house on the cul de sac. He didn't drive up the paved part to the garage, but instead drove up the gravel to the wooden fence. Quickly, he hopped out and opened the fence, then hopped back in and pulled forward. Soon the truck was concealed behind the fence.

"Does anyone live here?" Jaspierre asked.

"Of course nobody lives here. Do you think I'm fucking retarded? We will have to wait until dark, though."

"Why should we wait? There will be parents and stuff home at night. Wouldn't it be easier to take her now?"

"She ain't gonna open the door," Chance said firmly.

"And her parents will? When did opening a door worry you?"

He snorted. "I have visited her often enough that I know she doesn't particularly like me." He paused. "They've been really stepping up their game in security. The windows and doors are all alarmed, her room has bars. They have a safe room. She's gonna lock herself in there if we fuck this up."

Jaspierre rolled this around in her head. She was impatient to meet Lucille, but she wasn't expecting her to be afraid and angry in the first few moments they saw each other. She needed to revise her expectations quite a bit.

Chance opened the unlocked back door to the blue house. Jaspierre stepped inside, and quickly, but quietly, he pressed her against the wall. "Look here, we have time right now and I'll be damned if you make me wait any longer."

Jaspierre looked at him with a long, annoyed expression. "Lucille."

"In a minute. First, pay me what you owe." He started to claw at her shirt, demanding her breasts.

She burst out laughing. "Do you really think that I am about to allow this to happen? For all I know, you have driven me fucking nowhere and killed Lucille years ago. You have to fucking pony up." His hands gave up on the shirt, grabbing both breasts and squeezing them painfully through her clothes. "Now you will stop or you'll never be able to fuck again."

He cringed at the threat, his balls still aching from her last assault. He didn't bother to continue. "Fuck you. After we get her, I will tie you down if you make me. But you will give it."

"That's a lot of talk for a man whose balls I've crushed today," she said with a sneer.

He grinned and stepped back, giving her room to move. "Fine, let's come up with a plan and go get her then. I'm tired of fucking waiting."

She stood, staring at him curiously. "This has to be the most downright friendly we've been in a long time."

He burst out with a laugh. "I suppose so. Do you remember that time when we were kids? Before school, when we were running around outside like little maniacs."

"Yeah?"

"This one day you told me you were gonna marry me. You even handed me a little heart-shaped rock," he said.

Jaspierre laughed. "Are you making that up? I don't remember that."

"No, for real. We had to have been four or five. You were in a really fluffy skirt. It was before you had to go to work," Chance said, beaming.

Jaspierre's face fell. She remembered, before work. Before her first board meeting. When Mother was mostly absent, before she was hit nearly so much. Back when she was simply ignored. Those first four years were pretty good. It was the rest of them that were so damn hard.

"I might have said that, I dunno." She shook her head. "Do you think that everyone remembers their lives as before and afters? Before or after I went to work. Before or after I went to school."

"Before or after your first kill, right?"

Jaspierre laughed. "Well, there would be a

lot of before for me. I killed Katie and I was seventeen. I guess I was a bit of a late bloomer."

"Oh God, yeah, no shit. You practically had grey hair. I was ten, I don't even know why I waited so long. I have this friend in here in Canada, and he said he smothered his sister when he was three years old. Makes me feel ancient."

"Yeah, me too."

"Do you think Lucille has killed anyone yet?" Chance asked with an edge of prideful excitement.

I sure fucking hope not. Jaspierre cringed. The idea of her precious child turning into a murderer turned her stomach. She knew it was inevitable, but she still could hope that somehow Lucille wouldn't have to. That maybe she could just skip that awful part of life. Who was she kidding, though? It was a pipe dream.

JASPIERRE'S LAST CHANCE

CHAPTER

TWENTY-THREE

Jaspierre stared at the yellow house. Her patience was growing very thin. It had been four years since her baby had been snatched from her fingers. Did she still have blond curls? Chance wanted to wait until it was dark. He thought it would be easier. But if this family was jumpy, they'd be locked down tight at night.

So screw it. She was going to get her baby. *Now*.

"I'm gonna get her," Jaspierre mumbled and reached for the front door handle.

Chance immediately blocked her path with his foot. "No. We have to wait until it's dark. Someone will see us."

"You go ahead and fucking wait. I've done my waiting!" Jaspierre hissed.

His gnarled, scarred face twisted. "Fine. But

I can't go out there like this."

"Then you wait, you shithead." Jaspierre scowled at him.

He glared at her and nodded. "I'll be there the moment it's dark." She knew he didn't worry about her stealing Lucille and running off. He would find them again. Jaspierre didn't worry about it either; she'd kill him eventually, or he'd kill her. Such was the way of things.

Jaspierre stepped out onto the sidewalk, awkwardly aware of how out of place she felt. She was wearing her grey t-shirt dress, wrinkled from the long drive. The boots she wore had heels, and she was weaponless. What exactly would her plan be?

She wasn't sure. Get her daughter. That was the plan.

She walked slowly to the yellow house, watching the windows, noticing the little pink bike in the back yard. Her feet refused to move as she stared. Could Lucille ride a bike already? Somehow, it was feeling more real, and more painful. That bike sucked the air from her lungs and twisted her guts. Lucille could ride a bike.

Hot tears started to well up and she shook them off. Now was not the time to be emotional. Jaspierre had to be ready to fight, not cry. She clenched her fist. So much had been taken from her. From them! This time, she was going to get her back.

Her knuckles rapped at the door not a minute later. The knocking resulted in a long silence. She pressed the yellow glowing doorbell and the ringing was so loud she could practically feel it through the door. The door cracked open a few moments later. A thin boy, a teenager, cracked open the door just a bit. Jaspierre could see the chain was still attached. She couldn't burst in and take her daughter back. He had to unhook it first.

"Hello."

"Hi. What do you want?" the boy said, his eyes narrowed and suspicious.

"I wanted to talk to Lucille. Is she home?" Jaspierre tried to sound warm and friendly.

The boy's eyes grew wide and frightened. He shut the door quickly and she heard him lock it. Shit, now all she had done was tip her hand and let them know she was there. She slowly circled the house, finally stepping into the back yard. She could feel him watching her as she carefully tried each window. They were barred, not just shut and locked, but barred like a prison. She looked up at the pink curtain fluttering in the breeze. A curly blond head appeared.

"Hey, go away. I don't want you here," the

tiny little girl voice shouted down.

"I just wanted to meet you," Jaspierre said.

"Go away," the little girl replied. "You've been here too long. Peter is gonna call the cops. Go away."

"Do you know who I am?" Jaspierre said. "Come down and I'll tell you. I don't want to hurt you."

"You are bad. Go away." The little girl suddenly turned and said something into her room. Peter's head appeared in the window and shouted, "Leave. You have two more minutes, then I'm calling the cops." And the glass slid shut so fast the curtain was caught, a little tail flapping in the light breeze..

Jaspierre slowly walked back up the sidewalk toward the blue house. Why hadn't he called the cops right away? Maybe he wanted her to see how the house was tightly locked up, maybe he thought that would deter her. He was sorely mistaken. She was contemplating what to do next when a large red minivan drew up to the yellow house. The garage door very slowly crept open while the van waited in the driveway.

Now. Jaspierre's mind was a blur when her feet took off. The garage door opened all the way and the red van pulled forward. Jaspierre ducked inside after the mommy wagon, quickly pressing herself against the wall. She could feel her heart pounding and her breath was shallow. A woman with jet-black hair got out of the driver's seat. She was flicking at her phone, back and forth like it was no big deal. She opened the door from the garage to the house without unlocking it. The garage light turned off when she shut the door behind her.

Jaspierre crept to the door, listening in the dark for any sounds that might worry her. But she just heard normal family sounds. The mother was greeting the children and they made happy sounds to see each other.

Jaspierre opened the garage door slightly and slipped inside. She was in a hallway. To the left, it was dark, the lights all off besides a single night-light at ankle level in the hall. There were five doors, all shut.

To the right light flickered from a television and she could hear the quiet chopping in the kitchen of a woman making food. She slipped down the hall into the first door. It was a linen closet. The next was a small office, and then a bathroom. Another closet, and a large oddly shaped pantry. Jaspierre scouted quickly. She really wished she had a knife. A sword, preferably, but a knife at minimum. There didn't appear to be any knives sitting conveniently amongst the canned goods. There was, however, a rifle. Carefully, Jaspierre examined the gun. It was loaded and didn't have a gunlock on it anywhere. Jaspierre carefully removed the bullets and looked around for any others. It wasn't long until she saw the box sitting behind several bottles of ketchup. She took the box and dumped them into a box of old toys labeled "Donations." She had no intention of shooting anyone, but she also didn't want anyone to shoot her.

She pressed her ear to the doorway, and the low rumble of family life was down the hall. Nothing else. She carefully slipped out the pantry and into the dimly lit hallway. The kitchen seemed quieter, and Jaspierre could hear a woman speaking in low, soft mumbles to the boy. The empty rifle still clutched in her fingers, she stepped quickly into the kitchen. The kitchen was quiet and empty. Jaspierre quickly scouted the room and the large knife sitting on the counter was hers instantly. The open concept kitchen flowed out into the living room. Lucille was sitting on the couch, her blond curls shaking as she laughed at the pictures on the television. The television was not very loud, and Lucille's laughter was the only bright sounds in the room.

At the table on the other side of the kitchen island, the woman was leaning over Peter. Their

backs were to Jaspierre. They appeared to be
working on math- from their soft whisperings of
numbers. Jaspierre's heart was pounding so hard
she thought for certain they'd hear it. Jaspierre
quite quickly stepped forward and rammed the
knife through the woman's back. She pointed the
rifle at Peter. "Lucille, come here now." Lucille
turned, her blond curls no longer shaking with
laughter. "I'll shoot him if you make me."

The small child ran forward and grasped
the woman bleeding on the ground. Jaspierre's
brow wrinkled with confusion. Lucille started
screaming, "Mama! Mama!" bleating like a little
lamb, her voice loud and terrified.

Jaspierre shouted at the little girl, desperate
to be heard over the screams. "I am your mother!
Stop that this instant. We have to go home."

But the child did not stop. Lucille shook the
woman and kept bleating, "Mama, Mama" over
and over through wailing screams of horror.
Jaspierre could feel her blood boiling inside her.
What was wrong with this child? Had she not
seen a dead body before? Why couldn't she get it
together?

"She's dead. *I'm your mother*. It's time to go.
I'm rescuing you." She grabbed Lucille, but the
child somehow had super human strength,
dragging the dead woman as Jaspierre tried to

pull her. Peter stood frozen, dumbfounded and staring.

"Mama! Mama!" Lucille kept screeching.

Jaspierre couldn't contain herself a moment longer and slapped the child. "Is this the first dead person you've seen? Get it together! We have to go." Jaspierre could feel the dark hatred dripping off her tongue, but she couldn't control it. How dare Lucille utter "Mama" in front of her! How dare she? She had waited four years. *She was the mama.*

Lucille was stunned and went from screaming to sudden sobs. Her body changed from struggling and dragging the dead woman to limp. Jaspierre dropped the rifle and tossed her over her shoulder and marched towards the door. The sky was already growing dark. Chance would be driving up soon.

She heard a click as Peter aimed the gun and pulled the trigger. She turned her head slowly and looked at him. "I'm taking her. Now go do your homework."

Suddenly, Lucille was back to life, kicking and screaming. "Peter, don't leave me! Peter!"

Jaspierre couldn't concentrate with her child pummeling the shit out of her. It felt like she was carrying a baby gorilla, not a dainty four-year-old girl. "Enough!" Jaspierre's voice took on that familiar edge. The sharpness of Mother. Her hand cracked with pain as she slapped the center of Lucille's back. It stung like slapping concrete and the child let out a scream of pain. *Fuck. Shut up, shut up.* The words started to roar out of her. "Shut up, shut up! I'll do worse than slap you. Shut up!" Jaspierre clapped her own hand over her mouth, tears in her eyes. She had been a mother now for five minutes and had hit her daughter twice. Her soul cringed when she realized it.

Lucille shoved her hand over her mouth, terrified to be hit again. Jaspierre opened the front door. Peter still stood, terrified tears running down his face, the rifle limply pointed. "Don't take her!"

Just as she started to step out of the house, a large, muscular man stepped up to her and hit her in the face. A solid punch before she even had a chance to react. "Daddy!" Lucille screamed as Jaspierre and her daughter crashed to the ground in a little bed of flowers. The man towered over Jaspierre, charging forward, his fists cracking at her ribs and face. Jaspierre hit him hard in the nuts. Her fist finally found his jaw, *but he didn't even slow*. Her ribs cracked and snapped under the quick punch, punch, punches. Lucille crawled away, trying to get out from the scuffle. There was a loud shot and everything grew quiet. The man's head exploded. Jaspierre's ears were ringing. Chance stuffed Lucille into the truck while she screamed.

All she could remember was Lucas sitting next to her when his face exploded from the shot. His gorgeous blue eyes, and his soft voice when he asked her to marry him. When she agreed and his face exploded, his brains landing on her face. The moment all that time ago that still haunted her. When she still had little Lucille in her belly, she hadn't even known it yet. Lucas. Terror started to crawl through her body as the memory grew so strong it meshed with the reality. His face exploding. She shuddered with the pain, the fear, and held back her own terrified screams.

Chance lifted the dead man off of Jaspierre. Jaspierre let out a scream as she saw Chance lifting the man and for a moment of old panic, she started to scramble away. He wiped the brains off her face tenderly while she let out a sobbing sound. He stared at her and reached out his hand. "Come on, baby, let's go." Jaspierre took his hand.

Chapter

Twenty-Four

Peter frantically pounded on the passenger door before Chance drove off. "Let me come!" he screamed. "Don't make her go alone. Let me come."

Jaspierre rolled down the window her breathing still shallow, and her mind lost in memory. "What?"

"Let me come!" He had tears in his eyes. "Don't make her do this alone. Please."

Jaspierre gathered herself and finally looked at the boy curiously. "Why?"

"Please, I can be good. Please. Don't make her be alone. Please." He sounded desperate.

Chance pressed the button to roll up the window and started to pull forward. Jaspierre saw Peter, in frantic desperation, try to climb into the bed of the truck. Chance surely saw too, gunning it suddenly, causing the teen to topple off the back. She watched him in the side mirror, sobbing on the pavement while they drove off.

"Fuck, you are amazing," Chance said, sliding his hand up Jaspierre's dress. She pushed it away, but he pushed back. Finally, she gave up, staring out the window while he groped. She found tears welling up in her eyes. She kept trying to shake the memory of Lucas's beautiful face exploding. He would have been so mad that she slapped Lucille. Why had she done it! She was horrified. It had only been five minutes and already she was a terrible mother. Sirens were starting to whistle far behind them, but they'd be long gone soon.

Her hands pressed to her eyelids, trying to forbid the tears. Lucille sobbed in the back. Chance kept going, driving and grabbing her. This wasn't how she wanted to meet her daughter. She didn't want to scare her and steal her, and *hit her*. That was what Mother would have done. She hit, kicked, beat. Jaspierre was supposed to do better than that. Perhaps she could console the girl sobbing in the back seat. Jaspierre wasn't bad. She wasn't like Mother, she wasn't like Chance. She was a good person. That was a crazy situation. Jaspierre didn't think she would have to fight the child and Peter and her father all at once. How could she have done better? They had to get out of there before the cops showed up.

She pushed Chance's hand away and she could feel the heat of his stare. He wasn't even looking at the road, just staring her down with hate-filled eyes. "You owe me," he whispered in a harsh growl.

"I will make good. Where are you taking us? You're heading the wrong way."

"Home," he said. Jaspierre's stomach knotted up. She needed to go home, get her job back, raise her daughter, take care of her servals. Oh yes, and those damn people in the basement. She'd have to deal with them.

And Dru. She didn't know what she'd do with Dru yet. Too many questions to get rid of him. Would she even have time to coax the answers out of him while she had a daughter? The hand slid towards her skirt again. "Not yet."

"Dammit, Jaspierre!" His fist pounded into the dashboard. "I've been downright fucking nice to you, but my patience is gone." He grabbed her head and shoved it towards his crotch. "My patience! Is Mother. Fucking. Gone." And he thrusted his hips upwards on every word. "You owe me. You know you do. You fucking owe me!" He threw her head and it slammed into the steering wheel, beeping a startling honk.

"Lucille is in the car. I'm not gonna blow you while she is sitting right there," Jaspierre said calmly, trying to sit back up. Her head was ringing, her ribs were screaming with pain. But his hand grabbed her hair again, and he let out a scream of frustration, thrashing in his seat, slamming her head back and forth against him and the steering wheel. The horn beeped several times and the pain started to build in her head. It was already turning purple from the beating she received earlier.

"Goddammit, you fucking shit!" Jaspierre screamed back, her hands latching on to his throat. "I will pay you when I fucking want or, so help me, I will kill you." They heard honking as he swerved into the wrong lane. She released him and sat back in her seat. He drove angrily, speeding up, his eyes glued to the road furiously.

This was it. This was what Jaspierre had been training for all these years in prison. She knew that if they made it back to Chance's place, whatever it was, that she'd have one hell of a time getting out. He'd tie her up and fuck her and kill her. She had to kill him this time. She owed him that.

* * * * * * * * * * * *

It was growing dark, and Edward pulled off the road to hit a McDonalds. He was hopelessly lost. What the fuck was he thinking? He crammed fries in his mouth, and his anger-fueled drive was starting to wane. He couldn't possibly find her like this. He pressed both his hands to his temples and screamed *fuck* into the empty car. Tears were starting to burn his eyes as he twisted the radio dial, desperate to catch another crumb. Another body, or a car wreck or something happening now, here, near him. Something to give him a hint that he was in the right place. That he was gonna find her.

His knuckles crashed into the dash as he desperately tried to choke down the sad shit bubbling up inside him. A motherfucking monster had her. Jaspierre, this girl who grew up alone and lived alone and was locked in a cell alone. This person who needed love more than any other girl he had ever met. The woman whose fresh born baby he caught with his own two hands- and then was stolen from her. No wonder she was so fucked up.

And she was gonna die at the hands of a motherfucking monster.

He ran his fingers through his hair and took a deep breath. Not on his watch. He was going to save her and Lucille. He was going to do it or die trying.

He shoved the burger in his mouth and

started the car back up. He was just about to turn onto the highway when the radio let out a crackling scream. Home invasion, two dead, daughter taken: four years old with blond curly hair.

Tears did fall as he punched the roof of his car and squealed towards the house. He was gonna save them both.

CHAPTER

TWENTY-FIVE

"Why can't you love me back, dammit! You'll love anyone but me. What the fuck did I do wrong? I even kept your motherfucking bastard daughter safe for the last four years, and you won't even blow me as a thank you?" The car was starting to echo with his screams, but he didn't care. His own ears were ringing from the sounds of the blood rushing to his head, and the soundwaves bouncing between the windows.

"Fuck you! I've spent all these fucking years trying to make you love me, and you just have to fucking ruin everything. All the time, you fucking ruin it. Do you think I want to build you a goddamn torture chamber? Do you think that's what I want for you?" His breath was growing fast and furious. He punched the horn repeatedly and he could feel the car growing quieter and quieter while he grew bigger and bigger. His sounds, his feelings were starting to inhale the truck. The whole thing would explode if he wasn't careful, he would grow and grow and the windows wouldn't be able to hold him anymore. The seat already felt too small. He slammed his fist into the dashboard, then into the horn again and, again, the honking held him back. Kept him in the car. His body slowly deflated back to normal size.

But then he saw her and it grew again. "Do you think I want that for you!" His voice could no longer talk at a normal level, his sounds bulging as much as the truck must be. To hold him in, to hold in his strength, his fury, his terrible hate. And he did hate her; he hated her as much as he wanted to fuck her. She should fucking love him! Couldn't she see everything he did for her? He protected her from this violent, wretched world and yet she never saw it that way. She never would see it that way. She just saw him as a goddamn friend, not as a lover, not as a *man*.

He could shove his hard, massive cock down her throat and still she wouldn't see he was a man. If he split her in half from charging it through her so hard, she still wouldn't see what he saw. They had to be together. *She had to love him back.* If he didn't have a choice, then she couldn't have a choice. What kind of foul-mouthed bitch was she? How could she disrespect him? "Did you think I built you that room for no fucking reason? I know you don't get it, you just fucking don't get it. *We're together.*" The words dripped out of his mouth like venom off a snake. His gnarled, snarled, tattooed flesh pulled and tore as he strained it to its limits. Beyond its limits. He would go beyond all limits for her.

"Fucking hell!" His fist went cracking against the horn and the car in front of them skated out of the way. His foot pressed onto the pedal, shoving it tightly against the floor. Just as tightly as he wanted her slit wrapped around his dick. *Fucking fuck fuck.* "What is wrong with you! Can't you get it!" he screamed into the windshield, refusing to turn his eyes to meet hers. If he saw her eyes right now, he'd pull them from her skull and have them for dinner. She owed him. It was like watching her say yes to fucking Lucas's proposal all over again. It was like watching her refuse to wear his necklace.

Mine forever.

He wrestled the steering wheel so hard the console cracked. He was bigger than the car now, almost bigger then the planet. Swallowing the universe in hate. He could have been Hitler. With his bare rage, he could decimate millions, maybe even billions. Did she not see how the bullet shattered that man's face? As he pummeled Jaspierre into the ground, Chance rode in like a motherfucking prince and shot that bastard to pieces. *Was she even grateful?*

He let out a scream.

She said nothing; she said nothing. She couldn't, she wouldn't even apologize for being the hate-filled cunt that she was. Her left hand touched his fist just as it slammed into the console again. The cracks were starring across it further.

The warmth of her hand sucked him back in, back from the universe, back from the planet, back into the truck, sliding him normal-sized into the seat. She didn't recoil, holding him back in the truck, back from the space of time. He was the universe and yet, she could hold him with one touch.

He was wrong. *She loved him more than the sun loved the moon.* She could hold the universe back with one finger if she wanted. He let his foot off the gas pedal and the truck slowly released its death race. Eventually, it fell into pace with the other cars. "We're going home now," he said with firm warmth. She said nothing, for her power was too great. If she could hold the universe with one finger, then he couldn't imagine what her tongue could do.

But he couldn't wait to find out.

Jaspierre's Last Chance

* * * * * * * * * * * *

Jaspierre watched him spinning and spiraling. She could feel him. But she found a calmness inside of her. She was back in control of herself. She'd never lose Lucille again. Now she would find a way to keep them safe. She couldn't save them if she thought about Mother, or the way her hand slapped at her pretty daughter. So she abandoned her thoughts and instead focused on keeping them alive.

The only way to safety was to leave Chance before they got home. Before they got to the room he built especially to contain her. A room to subdue her. She knew what these kinds of rooms were like, having owned and placed many a person in that kind of room herself. She touched him and he grew quiet and calm. So she held his hand while building a plan. She stared out the window; it was all trees and snow. They were far north, and houses were stretching farther and farther apart.

Would Lucille set to screaming when they ran? Or would she understand? Jaspierre was her mother, Chance was her monster. Not some other version of what was happening. Was Lucille the same as Chance and Mother? Had her soul been twisted while she was being born?

Perhaps a good ironing would be all it

would take. Jaspierre closed her eyes. If only it was that easy to be undone and remade. Despite her best effort to keep her emotions at bay, a tear trickled down her cheek.

She glanced back at the child. At her child. *Lucille*. She was curled, unseat-belted, on the middle of the seat. Tears were still wet on her beautiful, perfect skin. She was sleeping. Jaspierre understood. Sleep was a way to cope. She tried not to remember sleeping in her closet with her baby serval when she was just a few years older than Lucille.

"Do you think I should make her put on her seatbelt?" Jaspierre asked Chance, resuming her staring out the passenger window. He shifted his grip, holding her hand warmly and sweetly.

"You're an amazing mother," he said dreamily. His words stung. *If only.*

She considered the sleeping child a moment more, then decided to let her be. It seemed extremely unlikely that the three of them in a car together would be in a major accident more than once. "Do you want me to drive? It's pretty late. Maybe you'd like to rest a little."

"I'm fine." He still had that dreamy look on his face.

When had she lost the knife? She meandered backwards in her mind. It was when that man socked her eyeball. She flipped down the visor, despite it being dark, and opened the little mirror. Two tiny little lights glowed at her face. Her left eye was swollen, almost shut, and her cheek was purple and blue. She shifted slightly, and the ache in her ribs hit her sharply for a moment. They were probably broken.

She thought being strong would have been enough to prepare her for this kind of shit. Wasn't that the whole damn point? She could be ready to fight Chance, yet somehow, she was utterly unprepared for that assault. This time, she wouldn't be holding Lucille while trying to fight hand to hand.

In fact, fighting hand to hand wasn't in the plan at all. Chance had a gun, or five on him right now. She could guess there were one or two under his seat, in the glovebox; she imagined the locked trunk in the pickup bed was all explosives, guns, or grenades. Hell, he had a rocket launcher the last time she robbed him. No, hand to hand combat simply wouldn't do. *You can't bring your fist to a gunfight.*

She'd already burned him alive, watched him be hit by a car, knifed him in the neck. What else would she have to do to kill him? What would she even do with herself once he was gone? He was right in that she gave him purpose. And he, in so many ways, had been a shadow on her entire life. Yes, she hated him, and he was dangerous and terrifying. But what would her life be like without him? It was hard to say.

When you are followed by a shadow, it's hard to imagine the light.

The houses had grown very far apart, being merely dots between large forests of trees. They were starting to climb up a mountain. The road was winding back and forth in tight, dangerous turns. Chance slowed down, and he was starting to look tired.

"I'm happy to take a turn driving; you can rest." At the very least, she needed him to stop the car. He shook his head. "Would you pull over and let me pee? I don't want to wet my pants, okay?"

He didn't even shake his head, just kept going.

So finally, she said the only thing that would make him stop. The only thing that would work.

She leaned in close, pressing her lips almost inside his ear. "Don't you understand, silly? I want to stop so I can blow you, but out of the car where Lucille can't hear." The car squealed to a stop moments later. There were three ways this could turn out. Jaspierre could win, kill him, steal the black truck and take her daughter home. Jaspierre could lose and end up covered in the semen of a man she hated. Or, worst of all, she could lose her life.

Jaspierre's Last Chance

CHAPTER

TWENTY-SIX

The gate to this community was wide open to allow the cops to freely drive in and out. Cop cars were everywhere when he arrived at the yellow house on the corner. They had covered the body on the front lawn with plastic. Edward stared at the mess and believed this was Chance. Jaspierre wouldn't, she couldn't murder these people who raised her daughter in cold blood. Peter was sitting on the porch steps. Edward recognized his face, older, but still the same boy that had been kidnapped years ago.

He had to be careful. He needed to figure out where the three amigos were headed and get on the road. It was not good for him to stick around and talk. Chance and Jaspierre were already on the road. He needed to go look now while the trail was still hot with blood. He grabbed a cop that was standing around looking at the crowd slowly forming. "I'm Detective Edward Darbonne. I need you to answer one question for me."

"I'm not answering questions." The cop didn't even lay eyes on Edward, scanning the crowd emotionlessly.

"Look, I have a hunch, and I want to check it out..."

Before he could continue, the cop cut him off. "You aren't able to come onto the crime scene, sir. Please back away."

"I don't want to come to the crime scene. I've been tailing these guys for a while. I think they'd probably go to some mountain cabins next. Is there an easy way to get to cabins from here? A main road? The kind of cabins with no electricity in which they could hide out a while?" Edward had a desperate edge grow in his voice. A sharp, desperate edge. The longer he waited, the farther away they would get.

The cop finally looked Edward in the eye. "A cabin?"

"I know this guy, I am just gonna take a drive and see if I can catch their trail. Point me to the road with the nearest cabins. That's it, nothing more."

"How do you know who did this?"

Suddenly, the cop's eyes narrowed and suspicion started to build.

Shit. He was gonna get taken in and questioned for hours if he wasn't careful. That would be the worst thing that could happen. Locked in an interrogation room answering pointless questions while Jaspierre and Lucille were dragged who knew where. "Is there a place like that nearby?"

Before the cop could answer, an older man gawking nearby suddenly said, "I'd start with St. Elmo's Road. It curls up the mountain to all sorts of desolate places. Hope you catch 'em. Take a left out of here, and just a couple of miles up, it's on the right."

Edward raced to his car before the cop could find a reason to hold him and question him. He drove fast, and impatiently, skittering on to St. Elmo's. He found himself driving faster instead of slowing down. He wished he could find something, a trickle of blood dripping out the back of their truck. No, not blood. He cringed. Something that would let him find them. Furious tears welled up again as he wound back and forth.

Nerves took hold and he slowed down. What if he had already passed them? What the fuck was he doing? Frantic driving was no way to catch a criminal. He had no plan, even if he did catch him. He stared back and forth down the road, trying to glimpse cabins between the trees. Why had he gone so far from home? He hoped, ridiculously, that he would see them getting out of their truck, or that Jaspierre would be running along the road with her daughter, both unharmed.

This was a fool's errand, but he had to try.

Uncertainty and fear crept closer, hounding his thoughts. Tainting his mind. She could already be dead. Lucille could be dead, Jaspierre could be dead. He might have passed them, they might be far ahead. *Face it, they're gone. I've lost them.*

Jaspierre's story would end this way, daughter of a mad scientist, stalked by a madman, killed before she had ever really had a chance. His emotions started to collide within him. He had been frantically driving across the country. What was he doing? Why did he think this would work?

His goddamned idea that he could ride up on a white horse and save her before it was too late. Saving her crashed his mind into a million pieces. Jaspierre deserved a little bit of hope so she could blossom into the good person he knew she could be.

He turned the tight corner and saw a truck on the side of the road. Chance, he was just sure it was Chance, was stepping out the driver's door, Jaspierre had just stepped out of the passenger door. Edward, without a second thought, pressed the gas, his bumper aimed straight at the man who was ruining their lives.

Jaspierre's Last Chance

CHAPTER

TWENTY-SEVEN

Her tongue lapping at his cock. Chance's brain couldn't register anything else. He hadn't even pulled off the road yet and his boner was raging in his pants. She would blow him so smooth and so fucking hard that he'd be calm for at least an hour. He doubted she had the masterful hooker skills he was used to, but he didn't need skills; he just needed her open mouth. The road swerved to the right, and he tore into the shoulder with the tires. They were fucking close to falling off this mountain road and down into the deep ravine below. He glanced over at her pretty little mouth. He couldn't wait to grasp handfuls of her hair and really give it to her. The trees were thick around the truck. His cock was stiff in his pants. She was going to blow him. Right here, right now. *Couldn't wait another second, could she?* Fucking delicious.

He opened the door and stepped out. The air was crisp and cool and delicious. *Fuck yes.* He turned to shut the door and a car slammed into his back, throwing him into the woods. The silver car caught the half-opened truck door, and the truck spun, the door crumpling. That was the last he remembered.

* * * * * * * * * * * *

Jaspierre had just opened her door, one foot already touching the ground when she heard the revving squeal. She was too far out of the truck to duck back in. She held on as the truck spun, nearly tossing her out the opened door. The door flipped shut against her, smashing her back and body as she dangled. Lucille screamed from the back seat. Her tiny body flung forward, unbuckled, into the seats, and she slid into the foot well. Her hysterical sobs rang in Jaspierre's ears. It was so hard to think when that child let her lungs fly free. It was so fucking hard to think.

Jaspierre pressed backwards as the truck rocked. The door opened again and she could breathe. Her ribs were *so* broken now. They screamed from inside her, grinding broken bits of bone together. She shut her eyes tight, willing her heart to slow enough that she could think. That she could run, or whatever she needed to do next.

What had happened?

The truck had moved somehow; with screaming crunching metal, it had spun. Where was Chance?

She couldn't see him anywhere. Another man was climbing out of the car. The sleek silver car. He tossed his brown hair back and was staring into the woods. Where was Chance? Chance should be fucking killing this man. She needed to take Lucille and run. Run. Motherfucking run. Her brain was aching with the desperate effort to find a plan.

Jaspierre ripped open the door and grabbed Lucille. Her tiny screams and violent kicks seemed much stronger than a four year old would be able to do. "Lucille, stop it! We can't stay here. It's not safe. Stop now! Don't make me!" Jaspierre's hand flew into the air, ready for a hard, painful slap. The child gasped with fear but grew quiet. Her entire body trembled.

She clung to Jaspierre suddenly. Jaspierre closed her eyes and held her daughter in a perfect, delicious hug. The child sobbed softy into her chest. "It's gonna be okay. But we gotta get somewhere safe."

* * * * * * * * * * * *

Edward stepped out of the car, his gun was drawn. He stepped forward, looking down into the woods. Chance had flown into a deep ravine between tree after tree. Edward could no longer see Chance. Was he dead?

Edward couldn't imagine he would be that lucky. Chance could survive a hell of a lot more than simple smack of a bumper. That said, he didn't hear any screaming, or anything to indicate life down there. So maybe he had gotten lucky? Maybe the monster was dead.

He turned and looked for Jaspierre, but he didn't see her. The wailing cries of the small child stopped. He heard a car door shut. He turned to see her sitting in his car. She threw it into reverse and the tires squealed. The car lurched backwards. She hadn't checked for traffic, and an oncoming car swerved around her, honking.

He raised his arms and waved them back and forth. He let out a scream, trying to get her attention, but she threw it into drive and squealed forward. He climbed into the passenger side of the truck since the driver-side door was completely mangled. The keys were missing. If they had gone down into the ravine with Chance, there was no way he could catch her. No way in hell.

Did she leave me on purpose? That very thought twisted in his gut.

He tried not to think about it. Surely, she hadn't seen him. If she had seen him, she would've waited. Maybe she just got frightened, trying to escape from Chance alive with her daughter.

Of course, maybe, not likely, but maybe she *had* done it on purpose. Maybe she had intended to leave him. Hysteria started to pound in his chest. *Maybe it was intentional.* She hadn't called him, or left a note, or invited him to help break out her servals.

What if she felt nothing? Here, he would run across the world for her. Risk his life, his badge. And she would leave him on the side of the road to battle a psychotic killer. *Shit,* he sure knew how to pick them.

Jaspierre's Last Chance

CHAPTER

TWENTY-EIGHT

Chance was sliding down rapidly. His fingertips grasped every branch, bush, limb; anything to try to slow his unyielding descent. He stopped suddenly when his feet collided against the trunk of the tree. Pain ricocheted up through his body, through his joints, through his bones. He looked up the long mountainous thing he had slid down.

At the top, he could see a thin man. The very man who had hit him with the car. It really fucking pissed him off that he was up there with his wife and child. He clawed mercilessly at the dirt in front of him, but he managed to make no progress. In fact, he almost lost his footing on the tree trunk and nearly slid farther down. That was the wrong direction.

She was just about to blow him too! He was

now fighting up a mountainside instead of being suckled. Exasperation bubbled up within his chest and he let out a real deep bellowing rage-scream.

He could hear the squeal of tires as some sort of angry reply. *Fuck*. Did that man take his wife? Rage rose up within him even stronger than before. He was frantic and clawed at the dirt, bound and determined to get to the top. To take his vengeance. To get back Jaspierre. He hadn't even gotten to screw her yet! She owed him. *She owed him!*

That fucking bitch owed him. He couldn't believe that they had been interrupted after all these years. She was willing, present, and owed him. Would a day like that ever exist again?

He didn't fucking think so. And whoever that man was fucked this up for him. And he sure as hell was going to pay. Chance found a small branch by his right hand and used it to drive into the dirt. He hoisted himself up a few inches. Grabbing another branch with his left hand, he dug it into the loose dirt. Using the two branches to puncture into the mountainside, he started to crawl upwards, scrambling his feet against the falling dirt. He was making frantic, angry progress. He'd be at the top in less than ten minutes.

* * * * * * * * * * * *

JASPIERRE'S LAST CHANCE

Edward stood at the top of the ravine, looking down nervously. Chance most certainly wasn't dead. The man seemed invincible. *Why the fuck had Jaspierre left him behind?* Had she seen him?

The truck didn't have keys in it. They were probably in Chance's pocket. Could there be a worse location? Edward stared down the road. He didn't hear any cars coming. He couldn't flag anyone down and get a ride. *Fuck.* He drove all this way, just for her. And she left him?

No. She didn't see him. She just thought there was some lunatic crashing into Chance. She didn't know, because if she did know, she would have stopped. He hoped that was true. He hoped that she would stop for him.

Of course, what did he really know of her? Maybe he didn't know anything. Here he was running across the country to save Lucille, to impress Jaspierre, to make something right out of this wretched world. He owed her; after all, he was there. He had caught the baby in his very hands. And then she had been stolen.

It seemed like so many of the hours of his life had been hinged on that very moment. That moment of regret that he couldn't get over, that he couldn't stop thinking about. It haunted him; it haunted his dreams and it haunted his waking hours. He would hear a baby cry and remember that it was his fault. He fucked up that little girl's life. He could never forgive himself for such a huge mistake.

Here he was, Lucille with her mother, and him with the serial killer. Chance was coming. Edward looked down the ravine and saw the man climbing the steep surface using sticks or something. *Holy fuck, he looked scary.* Terror swept through Edward's brain. His ability to formulate a plan was inhibited by the unrelenting fear. Chance was climbing the mountain, soaked in his own blood, covered in dirt. As Edward stared down at him, he heard the man's terrifying voice cry out, "You fucking wait for me. I'm gonna get you!" Chance's eyes, despite how tiny and far away they were, glinted with a terrifying sparkle. He was going to get up here; he was going to fucking kill.

Edward drew his gun and pointed it down the mountain. His hand was visibly shaking. He had fought a hell of a lot of bad guys throughout his career, but he had never been this scared. They never seemed so *invincible*. His first shot missed by a mile. He took a breath and closed his eyes. When he opened them, Chance seemed invigorated, faster. He was charging ahead like a bull. *Fuck*. Didn't he get winded?

He took his time and shot; this time, he was

steady, but somehow, he misjudged Chance's speed. The bullet was nearly an inch from his head. The dirt suddenly leaped right next to his face. Chance looked up, his glittering, terrifying eyes bright and clear. "Just stay put and I'm going to fucking kill you." His teeth seemed white, smiling at Edwards. He seemed so close already, Edward could start making out the gnarled snarls of skin on his face. The scars. The tattooed scars.

Edward found himself letting out a little shriek of terror as he aimed again. This time, the bullet managed to slice into Chance's flesh. It tore through his thigh in one side and out the other. Chance did a full body shudder in pain, but he didn't hesitate. He kept charging forward up higher and higher; he was getting too close. He'd be at the top in no time. Edward panicked, turned, and started to run.

Jaspierre's Last Chance

CHAPTER

TWENTY-NINE

Jaspierre almost stopped the car but resisted. Who was that? She might've stopped if she had known. But the only thing that was really on her mind was getting Lucille to safety and putting as many miles between her and Chance as possible.

He was going to follow her. He was going to kill her, kill Lucille. It seemed funny that someone she was so grateful for hours, or was it days ago? Someone she had kissed, on purpose, was the greatest enemy she'd ever had. Life was so confusing. What did she know of men, good or bad? The ones that stuck around were not the ones she wished would stick around.

The little car she was driving seem to be in good condition. The engine wasn't making any awful noises. The tank was three quarters full; that was pretty promising too. Where the hell should she go?

Home. That was where she wanted to go. Tessa and Ikali were waiting. Or, they'd better be waiting. Fuck, she had all those people in the basement, Dru still needed to be questioned, and Arnold had not yet proven himself to be loyal. Yet, there he was, captain of the ship. This was a dangerous way to live life, allowing such untrustworthy scoundrels to run free in her home. She had new cats to take care of, a lot of life to live, and her daughter to raise. Her eyes flittered to the little one.

Lucille was cowering in the passenger seat. She was afraid. Jaspierre rolled around in her mind something to say to reassure the little child. Finally, she settled on something her mother used to say. "You are fine."

Lucille looked up at her with big terrified eyes. They were wet with tears and fear. Lucille said nothing. She curled up and looked outside the passenger window, her little body trembling.

Jaspierre gripped the steering tightly, staring at out the window. Face it; she had already fucked it up. She'd never be a good mother. It wasn't in her genes. Her eyes welled up with tears. The first moment with her daughter and here she was, screaming at the child, scaring the shit out of her, and making her cry. *She even slapped the girl.* Just like Mother.

"Look, it's gonna be fine. You're going to be fine. You are fine," Jaspierre blurted out, struggling to maintain her composure. "You are a Kyller; we are Kyllers. Mother, Severina, was a difficult woman. And she is dead."

Lucille burst out a sob and shuddered at the word "dead."

"Wait, no. That's not what I meant. I didn't kill her. She is just dead. I don't know who killed her." Jaspierre had this sinking feeling that she was screwing up even further. There was a long silence and a few miles slipped down the road. "Severina, your grandmother, is dead. That's what I wanted to talk to you about. I wanted to tell you that she was a strong woman. She was unbelievably strong. One time..." Jaspierre stopped midsentence. She was going to say that her mother had cut off a man's ball during a dinner party. But that was the wrong thing to say. It would scare the shit out of this little girl.

"Okay, what I mean is, you have her DNA. So you are strong too. I'm strong. You can tell, because even after prison, I still managed to get you back, and Ikali and Tessa, and you and I escaped from Chance. So I'm strong. That's Severina's DNA, and that's your DNA." Jaspierre nervously looked over at the girl. She was still curled in a ball, tears running down her face. She looked terrified.

"Okay, so I don't know anything about you. Like not right now. Because I was in prison. I was wrongly convicted, okay? Shit, I am saying 'okay' too fucking much." Jaspierre let out an exasperated sigh and ran her fingers through her long hair. "Fuck, I don't know how to talk to you. You're just this kid." The car grew silent as Jaspierre stopped rambling.

Lucille was silent.

Another hour passed, and Jaspierre was getting really tired of it. "Do you have questions for me? I'm your mother!"

Lucille curled up tight like a turtle hiding further in its shell, hoping it would save her from the violent animal trying to tear inside the only protective layer that she had. Jaspierre felt the urge to hit her.

She shouldn't hit the kid. That was the worst part of her childhood, being smacked around, hit, beat, and punctured. Punctured by those sharp stilettos Mother was wearing. That particular red pair had a heel so tiny and so sharp that it would pop right into her skin with a sickening sound.

She didn't want to hit Lucille, but how else was she supposed to make the girl talk? She knew lots of torture techniques, but those were for people she didn't like. For people she didn't want to like her back. She should probably read a fucking parenting book.

"Do you want to eat?" It was supposed to be friendly question, like "Want to grab some milkshakes?" But it came out more like a terrifying command, laced with the dirty threat of starvation and terror. Jaspierre tried again. "Like, chicken nuggets? Or maybe ... I dunno... a burger? Are you a vegetarian?"

Lucille uncurled slightly and glanced up at her terrifying mother. She made one curt little nod and then curled back into a ball.

Shit. Was she a vegetarian? Or was she hungry? *Fuck*. Jaspierre drove up to the drive through McDonalds and wondered briefly how she was going to pay for this meal. She had no money with her.

They sat in line at the drive-through waiting their turn. Jaspierre frantically scrambled looking for change, a few dollars in the glove box, or, if she got really lucky, a credit card. She found a total of $8.32. When she finally managed to make her way to the ordering box, she stared at the menu uncomfortably.

$8.32.

What the fuck did you buy with that little

tiny amount of money? This was being poor, wasn't it? The car didn't seem to have any air in it. She had thousands upon millions upon billions taken from her, but no fucking way was she going to count change to buy a fucking hamburger. Her tummy rumbled, and she glanced at the little terrified girl next to her and ordered a Happy Meal. The lady kept asking her do you want fries, do you want apples, you want yogurt, you want milk, do you want nuggets, do you want a burger? After about a hundred questions, Jaspierre found herself screaming at the lady "I want a fucking Happy Meal. I want a fucking Happy Meal. No more questions!" Jaspierre struggled, her embarrassed anger taking over.. "Burger, fries, and Coke, and a fucking Happy Meal! No more questions!"

She revved the engine and pulled forward to make her point more clear. No more motherfucking questions. How were people supposed to order food for their kids when there were so many questions? What if she had two children? Or, God forbid, three children? It would be like four hundred or five hundred questions and Mom wouldn't have even ordered herself a hamburger. No wonder why raising kids was so hard.

They pulled forward to the window,

waiting in the slow line. Jaspierre struggled to maintain a sense of decorum. *Get yourself back under control.* She found her fingers rapping against the steering wheel as though it were a big obnoxious drum.

Finally, it was her turn at the window. There was a young lady with an overly high ponytail and a little sporty visor. She had plastered-on smile; it still looked a little nervously at Jaspierre. "That'll be ten twenty-five," she said. "Is this toy for a girl or boy?"

$10.25.

$8.32.

And, another mother fucking question. Jaspierre stared at the money in her hand and looked at the little girl in the car next to her. The air from the car was completely gone now and her lungs struggled to continue. And look at this stupid grinning girl with the overly high ponytail. There was a coldness ruling inside her.

For the very first time in her entire life, Jaspierre couldn't pay for something. In a split second, she handed the girl the money that she had. Jaspierre leaned out the car window, grabbed the bratty little lady's shirt, and screamed, "I said no more motherfucking questions!"

The room went cold and quiet as the little perky teller, obviously shaken, grabbed the little bag and the Happy Meal, shoved them in the car, and slammed the glass window shut.

Jaspierre pulled forward. She didn't get her Coke, she did not get her motherfucking Coke. And she didn't have another dime on her. Fuck. *Fuck Fuck Fuck.*

"Eat your shit," Jaspierre shouted, the rage still growing and brewing inside her.

Lucille pressed herself against the door so hard, she melted into it. The box with the Happy Meal crushed between her and the door, scooting as far away from Jaspierre as she could. Her trembling little fingers opened up a tiny burger in the meal and took a little nibble.

Jaspierre slammed on the gas; she needed to get home and get her fucking job back. She was too angry to realize how scared her daughter was.

Chapter

Thirty

Chance heaved himself over the top edge of the ravine. His side was aching; the bullet had grazed through chunk of his skin. He stood at the top, adrenaline surging within him. He felt, for a moment, that the whole world was feeding him energy.

Was that how the world worked? When someone was in greatest need, did it feed him? He was remarkably good, having just been hit by a car and thrown down a ravine and pierced by a bullet. He took a few steps. *Where had a little fucker gone?*

He looked to the left, then to the right. There was nothing to see, just instinct. His gut was screaming that he should go right, that the man was to the right. Right was the right way. With no further thought, just perfect decision, he followed

Edward. He was able to walk at a very quick pace, not quite running, but not quite *not running*.

He walked forward, confidence exuding from his skin. He'd catch the bastard. As he walked, the earth beneath his feet started to encourage him.

"He's just up ahead." The rocks rumbled an agreement. "Can you feel his footsteps?" The throbbing in his bloody thigh seemed to pulse with thoughts. "You are going to get him. You are going to get him."

His feet crunched on the ground, and the birds started to sing to him. "Up ahead. Up ahead." He could hear them screeching louder and louder, "Up ahead! Up ahead!"

Even the wind was starting to run with the scent of his prey. He could smell the man, his fear, and his weakness. The road was winding to the right, into the left, and into the right again. It was all switchbacks from here. They were going downhill, down the mountain. At some point, they'd find someone. But not before it was too late.

He rounded the final bend, and there Edward was sitting. He looked tired. His eyes lit up with fear as he glanced up and saw Chance. He scrambled, gun drawn, frantically backing up. And the whole world waited a moment, taking a deep big breath, and in that inhale while Edward was scrambling, Chance charged forward.

* * * * * * * * * * *

Edward scrambled backwards with his feet, trying desperately to catch himself. He wasn't ready; he had been dozing. He was sleepwalking in drained zombie fear. His brain was grinding, screeching to a halt. *Shoot him!*

His brain kept screaming, but his hands were utterly useless. They flailed like a little girl's, not like a trained officer. *Shoot him!* How had he found him so easily? How had he caught up at all?

Edward had been running, crashing ahead in delirious fear. He had sat down, just a moment earlier, catching his breath. He should've been ten minutes ahead, maybe even twenty. The man had fallen down the ravine! How had he climbed out so quickly?

Edward's brain crashed. None of his limbs would work right. Fear froze him. *This can't be happening. Shoot him! This can't be happening! Shoot him, you fool!*

And just as his hand finally made its way to the gun, raising it at Chance, the serial killer, the blemish, the embarrassment of his precinct, and his finger made contact with the trigger, he was thrown to the ground.

The two men wrestled, but it was quickly clear that Chance was far superior. He was stronger, more powerful; *he was invincible.* Edward frantically tried to drive the gun into Chance's mouth so he could pull the trigger and end it, end it finally.

Edward tried everything he was trained to do; he tried everything he wasn't trained to do. He tried to survive. But somehow, in the struggle, Chance had the gun. And before Edward could do anything more, the handle slammed into his skull over and over, again and again, until finally, the world went dark.

CHAPTER

THIRTY-ONE

"What have you done!" she shouted. Jaspierre grabbed the chain, yanking it out harder, and higher and higher Dru lifted in the air. Then he fell.

"How! How did you transfer my shares to you? How did you do this to my job? How did you do it?" she said.

Dru made incoherent gurgling noises as blood dripped from his mouth and he dangled at the bottom of the chain.

"You." Her finger pointed, pressed against his forehead, pushing his dangling head back so that he could look her in the eyes. "You. Will fix this." She sat on the floor in the middle of the room.

She had just gotten back from meeting with her attorney and speaking with the board at Kyller and Co. Lucille was still locked in her bedroom, still unwilling to say a goddamn word.

They had been home about one day, maybe two. Jaspierre couldn't be bothered to keep track of time. Her ribs still ached from the cracked beatings she had received, but her face was remarkably less black and blue already.

"How did you do it." Jaspierre didn't really ask a question. It was more command: *you fucking tell me. You will fucking tell me.*

Dru slowly smiled. "Why would I sign it back to you?"

Jaspierre let out a little scream. She was like a small child teetering on the edge of a temper tantrum. The only way her temper tantrum would end would be in Dru's evisceration, his death, decapitation, and gut removal. She still had managed a bit of self-control and did not bring a sword into this room. Or else. Or else she wouldn't be able to contain the feeling, contain the rage. She counted to ten slowly.

In fact, her only weapons she allowed in here were her fists and the chain. But those were more than enough. Dru probably wouldn't survive his current injuries, much less when she added to them. And she wanted to, oh, she would. Even if he told her how he had done it, even if he returned to her to the glorious position of wealth her mother gave her. Kyller and Co. was Severina's and he stole it. She had been stolen from! This kind of backstabbing betrayal was not something that Jaspierre could handle.

Severina never handled betrayal well either. She would've done worse, much worse, damn the consequences. But Jaspierre had Lucille. Jaspierre was broke and needed her money back. So she couldn't just willy-nilly slaughter the man just because he betrayed her. No, she had to get it back first.

"Tell me." She was now sitting on the floor in front of him cross-legged with her hands pressed tightly together in her lap. Her eyes were shut. Breathing hurt as her ribs ached from all the effort she was putting in. She didn't need to look at him; he could answer the question just fine with her eyes shut.

"Let's go, Dru," she said again.

"What's in it for me? What do I get if I tell you? Nothing. You might as well die a pauper like you deserved from the very fucking beginning." Little drops of blood flickered as he spat angrily at her. "Severina grew up with family money. What the fuck did she know? You grew up with the same tainted blood money. You never earned a damn dime in your life. You don't deserve it."

"I don't have to deserve it. I just have to be

born into it. Is that what this is? You're angry that your parents worked as cashiers or some dumb shit? You're angry that you lived under a bridge when you were two? You're angry that you can't carve your own goddamn path?" Her hands twitched in her lap, begging for the chain. Begging to drop him once more, once again. Let him fall, let him cry, let his guts twist inside his belly and explode. "Whatever Severina did to you doesn't matter, she isnot me. I didn't do that. I am absolutely sure that you aren't the worst person she betrayed. You aren't even the most fascinating or interesting. She talked, killed, and screwed so many goddamn people, you aren't even on her top ten list."

Jaspierre stood up. The twitching in her hands was unbearable; she really wanted that chain. *Ring that bell.* "However, you make *my* top five." She leaned in close, her eyes boring into his, their noses almost touching. His mouth was still dripping blood. "Are you sure you want to keep pissing me off? Because you aren't hurting Severina. You aren't hurting me. You," her hands grasped the chain and slowly started raising him, "are only hurting yourself."

Dru let out a scream; she had barely had lifted him more than a foot. And there he was, screaming like a fool. *Scream, Dru. Scream.* She

234

held him there, one foot up, and he started to panic. His body thrashed around, dangling on the chain. She pulled a little harder to raise him up a few more inches. Suddenly, just like that, he changed his mind. She wasn't sure if it was just torture, or if it was her excellent speech. But he finally cried uncle.

"Stop! Please. I can, I will do it." His voice was hoarse and his body writhed with pain. "I'll get you the company. Please stop."

"Okay." Jaspierre gently lowered him down, careful not to jar his swelling body. She pressed her hand onto the wall, and a small panel slid open. Inside the box was a leather portfolio. She slid it out, opened it up, and took out a pen. Inside the leather portfolio was the three-hundred-page contract at her lawyer had drafted up. "Don't you dare drip a drop on those papers."

He had to initial thirteen different pages and sign four different copies of the final page. But he did it without dripping a single red drop.

Jaspierre's Last Chance

CHAPTER

THIRTY-TWO

Jaspierre sat at the head of her boardroom. It was nice to be back in the place where she belonged. Her bank accounts, so weak and weary, were filling up slowly with cash.

Lucille still hadn't said a word and locked herself in her room. Jaspierre put her directly next to her, next to Lucas's room. She hadn't gone and visited the girl much at all; it had been three, maybe four days. She wasn't sure. She had been busy getting her company back, making sure she had a legacy for Lucille. But embarrassment was strong when she thought of the child. What if she couldn't stop herself from hitting her?

There had been a great many changes while she had been gone. For instance, the division of medical equipment had been expanded greatly, including newer versions of many different types of medical 3-D printers. It seemed Dru was getting quite enthusiastic about them.

The pharmaceutical side of things had been dropped significantly. They lost two of the largest clients in the last few years to companies that were more responsive to their needs. Jaspierre and the board discussed strategies to gain them back, something Dru never even discussed, claiming that if they don't want us, we don't want them.

Lucille still had not said a word.

Jaspierre had a little inkling of fear every time she thought about her daughter. Maybe she was terrible mother. Was this what motherhood was like? Trying to make money at work, but rogue thoughts flitter back to your beautiful daughter? Trying to focus on medication business strategy, focusing on the bottom line, and still thinking about your mute baby girl? Jaspierre had been planning to stay late, working late. She did that whenever she wanted before. But now she was a mother.

She got home quickly and strutted up the marble steps into the grand foyer. Arnold stood in the foyer, staring at her. "What do you want to do with the people in the basement?"

"I will decide tonight. Is she...?" She nodded toward the stairs.

"Yes," he said.

Jaspierre's Last Chance

Jaspierre clicked her long heels up the stairs, past her ruined bedroom on the right, past Lucas's room (*which she was staying in*) to the next little bedroom, which was Lucille's.

She almost knocked on the door, but that was not what a mother would do. Instead, she swung it open. Lucille was under the bed, curled into a ball. It sounded like she was crying again.

"Lucille. Out from there. I have something to show you." The child did not move. "Don't make me come get you!" She cringed at her own threat as soon as she said it. Slowly, the little blonde curls started to creep out from under the bed, and finally, after they appeared, the tiny scrawny little four-year-old body also appeared.

"Come." Jaspierre almost grabbed the little girl's hand, then changed her mind. She marched the child in front of her like a prisoner. They walked downstairs, one after another. Lucille was timid, but Jaspierre strode confidently through the foyer and toward the pool. "Have you seen the pool? No, you haven't, because you won't get out of your room."

"Come." She pulled her to the left, to a large set of wooden doors. "Quickly; we can't let them out." She grabbed the girl, creaked the door slightly open, and shoved her in the room. She slipped in behind, latching the door behind her. "I haven't named them yet."

The room was stuffed to the brim with play equipment. Slides, rope ladders, balls, a swing set; but who could even look at those things when there were servals everywhere? The mother was licking the few kits. Ikali and Tessa curled together on top of the playhouse. And the rambunctious teenager was wrestling a ball.

Lucille's eyes grew wide, but she still said nothing. She crawled nervously over to the teenager. His ears perked up and looked at her.

"You can name them. Except for Tessa and Ikali, those two." Jaspierre pointed. "The rest are yours. You must feed them, water them, whatever else children do with these creatures. Teach them to be nice; don't let them hurt you."

Lucille said nothing but eventually started petting the teenager. He curled under her fingertips, gloriously beautiful. She kissed him but still said nothing.

"You could say thank you. I just gave you a really cool present. Do you even understand? These are thirteen-thousand-dollar cats!" Jaspierre's heart start to pound as the rage started to build within her. "You may play with them later; right now, we will do something else." She dragged the girl by her arm and charged her out of the room.

Jaspierre's Last Chance

"Do you know how to swim?" she asked as she trudged towards the pool, dragging the sobbing little girl. "Do you know how to swim? Can you!" She threw the girl into the water with a loud splash. Lucille let out a crying scream, but no words. Not a single word.

"Just say anything! Say anything!" Jaspierre's voice grew hot and loud.

Jaspierre watched as her daughter struggled to keep her face out, thrashing in the waters, struggling and slowly realizing her nose was still below the water, her frantic eyes begging for mercy. But her nose was below the water.

"Say anything, and I'll get you out."

Jaspierre watched as she struggled and struggled, growing quieter and quieter as she could not get her nose out of the water. Jaspierre turned her head in disgust, furious that the stupid little child wouldn't talk. Why wouldn't she talk!

The little girl cried as she drowned. Tears leaked into the pool as she struggled to survive.

Arnold walked in and let out a scream. He dove into the water and pulled out the child. She wept in his arms as he held her. "What the fuck is wrong with you, Jaspierre! Don't you want her to like you? You're her mother. You are supposed to protect her from the nasty shit in the world, not dump more on her." He picked her up and kissed her forehead, turning to the child. "Your mama doesn't know what she is doing." And he carried her up to her room.

Jaspierre watched, the rage somehow dissipating within her. She just wanted the kid to talk! She just...

He was right. She was fucking it all up. How could she do better?

Chapter

Thirty-Three

The phone rang several times before finally his message beeped.

"This is Detective Darbonne, please leave a message." Beep.

"Edward, I think I might need to see a therapist. I have all the stuff from my mom and now that Lucille's here, I can't seem to be normal. I don't know, maybe prison just changed me more than I thought. We should be sitting together reading a book, doing mom and daughter stuff. Getting ice cream, but instead, instead, we're having all sorts of trouble. She won't talk to me. I don't mean, like she won't talk personally to me. She won't talk to anyone. I'm starting to wonder if she's gone mute." Jaspierre stood with the phone pressed to her ear, pacing back and forth around her room.

"I just, I just don't know how to help her. I keep getting angry, and I didn't think I would be so angry. But every time she looks at me with those mute sobbing eyes, I keep thinking about all these years and how she's been ruined. I was locked up and somebody ruined her. It makes me so angry. I don't know what they did to her, but I can't reverse it. I wish you would call me back." She hung up the phone. She paced quickly, back and forth in her room. Edward hadn't called her in a few days. Maybe he didn't enjoy their kiss.

She stepped into the hallway and turned to Lucille's room, but hesitated. Her heart hurt. How could she be a good mother when she was full of so much anger? Her whole world was ruined. She thought she'd die avenging her daughter. But now... now Lucille was alive. Why was it so hard to connect?

Jaspierre could do better. She would do better. She walked away from Lucille's door and went out. She came back an hour later, arms full of parenting books, and sat in her room, sniffling and reading.

* * * * * * * * * * * *

Arnold, Jaspierre, and Lucille sat together at the long, winding table. Jaspierre was hoping a family meal together would really inspire the child. She'd find something brilliant to say, like

"Thank you for this frozen lasagna." Jaspierre still wondered if the child was a vegetarian. She picked at her food, but it never seemed clear if she was picking out meat or just picking away like a child did. If she would talk, then they would know, wouldn't they?

"Ma'am, what would you like me to do with the people?" Arnold said, carefully eating his food in order. He had sorted lasagna into sauce, cheese, noodles, meat. He was eating them one category at a time. Jaspierre suddenly remembered about his fetish of sorting people by organ size. He was a very odd one.

"What do you think we should do with them?" she replied, crunching through the crisp garlic bread. "I would kind of like to release them..." She chewed thoughtfully. "I mean, I don't have a beef with them or anything. I just can't figure out what to do with them. I don't want any of this reflecting badly upon us."

Lucille sat quietly four chairs away. The table snaked around the room like a long coil. It had tiny little planks like a little tiny railroad track running down the center of the table. Jaspierre set the basket of garlic bread on the tiny little planks and pressed the button. The little conveyor belts chugged forward, sliding around the table, bringing the basket to Lucille.

"If you want more bread, take it." Jaspierre looked at the child. All the anger of the years being locked up, all the anger of the years that she missed with her own flesh and blood. Wasn't she supposed to feel loved? Wasn't she supposed to feel happy? She took a deep breath and tried to remember the book about positive parenting. "I hope you enjoy it." She tried to smile at the girl.

"I can see the dilemma. But either way, they need to be dealt with. People live too long to just keep them in your basement indefinitely." Arnold carefully ate the cheese. He was just about to start in on the noodles. "I don't think you should let them live. I don't know if anyone is looking for this particular set of people, but I do know that these people are going to tell if you let them out. They aren't going to complacently go back to their sorry little lives with an elephant nose attached to them. They can't." He lifted his fork and pointed it at Jaspierre.

"I know, but I get tired of senselessly killing people. Besides, the corpses burning in the fireplace are so potent. It would be weeks of burning flesh, maybe even months, there so many of them. I just don't want to smell that gagging wretched scent day in and day out." Jaspierre took another bite of the steaming lasagna.

"Well, if you don't care how I do it..." He

struggled to hold back a grim smile. "It would be nice to have some order back in the world." His voice trembled on the word "order." She knew that he was itching to start counting one two three four, tapping his fingers to thumb to finger over and over in a repetitive motion.

"Are you going to torture them? Or will it be a comfortable end to their pitiful lives?" Jaspierre could feel the coldness in the room as she said it. It was like the air was being sucked out of her lungs. She could hardly stand it. Just slaughter those ten or so people. Because they were inconvenient. She pushed away her plate of food and kept staring at Arnold's perfectly organized lasagna.

"Lucille? Do you have anything to say about the matter?" Jaspierre turned to her daughter, who was sitting several chairs away. The child did not look up. "Should we release or kill the people in the basement? Should they live? Or should they die? Pay attention. If you say nothing, ten people that Dru attached parts of animals to will die. If you tell us to let them live, I'll release them in a desert or something. Just say something." Her voice had a soft pleading to it. One of the parenting books she had read said the importance of giving children a choice. Two options, and let them choose to avoid conflict. One example was two shirt, so they'd still put a shirt on, but they got to pick which shirt.

Arnold and Jaspierre turned and stared at the girl sitting down the table. The four-year-old's curly blond hair hung in front of her face, almost dipped in the lasagna. She pushed her plate away from her and started to sob, her face pressed on the wooden table and her arms curled around it.

"I am not sure she knows what you are talking about. After dinner, let's go down and show her, and then she will decide. If she speaks, they live. If she is silent, they die." Jaspierre stood from the table and shoved her chair in. "Arnold, clean this up. I'll be back in fifteen minutes." She could feel the rage burning inside her. She was angry there were people in her basement to deal with at all, she was angry her daughter wouldn't speak, she was angry that all these years had gone by and she had been betrayed in so many ways. But somehow, Lucille represented every ounce of that anger. Lucille's pretty blonde hair looked like Lucas's. Lucas, the only person who had ever given her love. And now she was fucking it up for the kid and fucking it up for herself. She couldn't seem to stop.

She ran upstairs and tried to collect herself, splashing water on her face and flipping through her parenting book. It definitely said that giving her two choices would help.

Maybe, in a moment, Lucille would say something to her. Maybe she would tell her to stop. "Stop being so angry, Mommy." Maybe that was what she was waiting for. Well, they would sure see in a moment.

Jaspierre's Last Chance

CHAPTER

THIRTY-FOUR

Edward woke up, lying in an alleyway. *How did I get here?* He was wrapped in a green military-style blanket. It was scratchy; his first sensation was the scratchy blanket. Gradually, as he awoke more fully, he became aware of the pounding in his skull.

He could hear cars. Slowly, they came into focus. He sat up gingerly, looking around. He was next to a green dumpster with the paint peeling. The stench of something rotting slowly curled up his nose. He wasn't sure what was happening.

He heard another car pass by. As he looked, the light at the end of the alley went dark and then bright again. The road was right there. His whole body was shaking, trembling from-- cold? Was it adrenaline? He wasn't sure. He felt bad. There was a sick sensation in the pit of his stomach. There was that odd emptiness in his throat, deep in his throat. The same feeling you get after you have been vomiting profusely. He looked vacantly at the blanket, but he didn't see any vomit.

His brain was sludgy through muck and mud. All of his thoughts were blurred together, and another car passed by. Dark, then light. His mind latched on to one thing, the one thing he needed to remember. He needed help. Instinctively, he didn't try to get up. He was hurt, somewhere. He hadn't quite figured out where yet. Maybe his kidneys were gone. Something was gone.

He scooted slowly towards the light. Dark, then light. This was a busy alley. No, the street was busy. The alley was quiet; it was just him. He wondered briefly if he should just throw himself in front of the car. Either they would help him and he would live, or they would crush him and he would die. Both options seemed equal. They were somehow the same option.

He finally made it to the sidewalk. He hadn't stood up, just scooted slowly. A grown man in a suit and tie paused when he saw Edward lying on the sidewalk. He didn't say anything; he didn't say, "Can I help you?" He didn't say, "Do you need a hospital?" He said nothing; in fact, he crossed the street.

Edward suddenly burst into frightened tears. What if no one would help him? What if they would all leave him behind, like Jaspierre did.

Jaspierre left him.

"Help." His voice was foreign, and his throat scratchy, like he been screaming. For a flicker of a moment, he remembered screaming. But he tried to forget it.

"Help. Call 911. Attacked." It was so hard to breathe. Were his lungs working? He closed his eyes and inhaled slowly, then pushed the air out slowly. It burned. He could feel a little rattle in his lungs. Frightened tears slowly turned back to anger. Jaspierre left him. Why did she do that? She knew what Chance was. She knew what would happen to him! If he had known, he would've never gone after her.

He took another deep breath and tried to get to his feet. But the pain started screaming up his body. The pain stole every thought from his head. It was so severe, he left his body for a full minute before he came crashing back down from the clouds. A man standing on the streets in a red hoodie looked over at Edward while he screamed and fell back to the ground. "You okay, man?"

With a gasping sob, Edward cried out,

remembering. "He took my toes."

CHAPTER

THIRTY-FIVE

The walk through the office was silent. Jaspierre reached up and clicked the ear of the still broken serval statue. Arnold didn't say anything; he was staring at the small girl standing between them.

The fireplace swung open, and dark dungeon stairs were smoothly revealed. Jaspierre clicked the light. There was one long window on the left near a huge control center. On the right there were three smaller windows. She looked into the maze, the white panels were still in funny shaped boxes to serve as rooms or houses or whatever for these people. In the rooms on the right, there were still the occupants: Dru, the angry man, and the girl with the wings.

"Can you see?" Jaspierre looked at the little girl. She reached down and picked her up, holding her in front, sitting on the rail like an exhibit at the zoo. Lucille's eyes grew wide as she took in the scene. The white floors, the white walls, the white boxes. That man with an elephant nose stitched where his human one should've been. She stared at the snake breasts of the lady dragging on the ground around her. She started breathing hard, little hands trembling, scared little four-year-old. Her headstarted shaking , the curls flipping back and forth across her now tightly shut eyes.

"These are people. They probably have children, definitely have mothers and fathers who love them. These are regular people that Dru has attached body parts to. Do you understand? That man," Jaspierre tapped the glass," with that long elephant nose; he is a person. He's been tortured. Dru printed up that crazy-ass nose and sewed it to his face. It's not his real nose; he didn't grow it. It's glued on, let's say."

Lucille said nothing. Her eyes were wide, and she had tears again. *Again, with the tears.* Had she figured out that Jaspierre wasn't the kind of mother to cow to her little tiny leaking face?

"The problem is that people who have been tortured and left in your basement to rot are hard to get rid of. You have two choices: you can execute them, kill them, or you can release them and risk that you will go to prison. So which to choose? Should I execute--kill, just to be clear, I mean kill them--or release them? If you say nothing, they die. All of them. Arnold will take them apart like he did the lasagna. Sort them, then we will burn and bury and whatever the hell we have to do. And you will help. I helped burned bodies when I was your age, and it's never too young to learn. You never know when you're going to need to learn how to burn a corpse. And if you are in some sort of terrible rush and don't know how to do it, then that's a failing on my part. You aren't prepared for this world, Lucille. When your grandmother was your age, she had already killed and disposed of the bodies herself. You struggle just with talking. *Talking.*" Jaspierre tapped the glass again frantically with her fingertips. "You are helplessly behind because I was in prison. So you, you are going to make your first grown-up decision, Lucille. Say nothing, they die. Say anything, and I will set them free and take that risk for you."

Lucille's wide eyes stared back through the window at the man with the elephant nose, the women, the men. She didn't say anything, but her tears finally stopped.

"I will count to three. And then, you choose. Do you understand me?" Jaspierre said.

Her anger had finally faded into that calm, collected feeling, the feeling she got right before she ran a blade through the gut of an angry man. This is what those parenting books suggested, two choices.

"One."

Lucille stared into the glass.

"Two."

A single tear rolled down her cheek.

"Three."

Lucille turned and looked at her mother. She said nothing. She didn't even try.

Instead of feeling angry at the perpetual silence of her only child, Jaspierre found herself grinning. She made her choice; she could have said no. She could have shook her head, she could have screamed. The child knew how to scream. No, this was her decision. She had made a good one. She didn't want Jaspierre in prison; she wanted to stay here. She wanted to learn how to bury a body, how to cover it with wood, and how to bear the stench of burning flesh.

"Welcome to the family, Lucille."

CHAPTER

THIRTY-SIX

Jaspierre sat quietly in Dru's cell. She sat on the floor, staring up at him. He was still chained to the wall, although Arnold had fed him and watered him recently. He still dangled like a puppet.

"Tell me about Mother," Jaspierre said. "How did you convince her to marry you?"

"I was young. She was young," he said slowly. "It would be much easier to tell you these things if you let me off this goddamn wall!" His voice took on a sharp pitch, and he was angry.

"Why?" Her eyes grew slanted and irritated. "What would be the point? Either I'm going to kill you now, or you are going to tell me the goddamn story. Then I will kill you later."

She wanted to know. But she didn't want to deal with Dru any longer than necessary, and if he was going to tell her, so be it. She never knew Mother was married. She never *knew* Mother. But she had Lucille and her job back, and there really wasn't anything left. Besides a story. Just a story.

Then why did she want it so bad?

"Just tell me."

"Why should I tell you when you are going to kill me either way?"

"I kept Lucas down here for what, ten years? You can have time left if you choose."

He let out a cackling laugh. "You sure didn't fall far from the tree. Was Lucas your brother? Your uncle? Let me guess. You two fucked."

"What the hell are you talking about?"

His chains rattled as he laughed harder. "She never told you? She never told you! Jasper was your uncle. Don't you know that? You incestuous creation. You sick little bastard." Jaspierre's face grew pale as he continued. "I married Severina when we were very young, and she didn't tell me that she had him in the basement. Much less that she was fucking him. It kind of pissed me off when I found out. I missed out on all the goddamn fun!" His chains were rattling as he was laughing and shaking and thrashing in them. "I helped her build this empire! Viscardine was mine. I helped her hire the people, *the right kind of people.*" He twisted his tongue in his mouth, biting it. He was gloriously furious. "Everything you have is because of me. You deserved nothing, you incestuous bastard." He tried to spit on her, but she left the room.

He howled with fury, completely unable to contain his rage. "You owe me! She owes me! You fucking Kyller. You dirty bitches! I should have killed you when I had the chance. Severina sent me to prison, goddamn prison. After everything I did for her!" His screams echoed in the empty room, bouncing back against the white walls.

Jaspierre opened the door again, and she stood there with a long sword. She stepped forward and the tip of the blade rattled against the ground behind her. She didn't move, staring at him with a hateful glare. "He was not my fucking uncle." And the blade sang through the air as it ripped off Dru's head. She left it rolling on the ground, and she went back up the spiral staircase. *He was a fucking liar.*

JASPIERRE'S LAST CHANCE

CHAPTER

THIRTY-SEVEN

Jaspierre stood outside Lucille's room. She wanted to talk to the child, but she found herself hesitant. Finally, she threw open the bedroom door and poked her head inside. Lucille was under a blanket, curled in the ball.

Fuck. She was crying again. Jaspierre stepped into the room and sat awkwardly on the very edge of the bed "Lucille? I-I wanted to apologize for throwing you in the pool. I don't know what I was thinking."

The little blonde curls lay out from under the blanket and her tiny blue eyes looked up at Jaspierre. The blue eyes looked just like Lucas's.

"Honey, I don't know how to be a mom. Severina, your grandmother was..." Jaspierre paused. What was Severina? Tough. She was powerful, she was... She was really bad. "Mother didn't show me love. She didn't show me anything. Mostly, she just... was very bad. She hit me, she killed lots of people."

Jaspierre looked down at her hands, then back at the big blue eyes staring at her. "I haven't learned how to be a normal mom to you. You got stolen from me before I could learn anything. If we had those years together, I would already be better, and you would already understand me. But now we skipped ahead. And while you were growing, I was growing angry. I waited in a prison cell for years. I waited for your whole life, just to defend you. I was going to kill Chance--you know, the man with the face." She gestured on herself to where the scars that littered Chance's face would be. Lucille's eyes grew wide and she scrambled backwards on the bed. She knew Chance. She knew him.

"I can kill him if you want me to." Lucille frantically nodded. "I am sorry. I don't want to be this angry person. I don't want to throw you in the pool, or slap you, screw you up any worse." Jaspierre's own hot tears fell. "Just give me a chance. And I will learn to be a good mom. I even got parenting books. They have this thing called peaceful parenting, where we don't yell and I give you choices. It's supposed to let you have control and me have control. I think that's going to help.

We're in this together."

Lucille very nervously reached out a tiny little hand and put it on top of Jaspierre. She was still silent, but that little touch made Jaspierre feel so much better. Jaspierre suddenly hugged the little girl. Lucille hugged her back tightly. And for the first moment, Jaspierre suddenly loved the little girl. But right then, the bedroom door opened.

"I need some help," Arnold said. There was a sense of urgency in his voice.

JASPIERRE'S LAST CHANCE

CHAPTER

THIRTY-EIGHT

"I'm sorry to tell you, Edward, but you probably already know. We can't..." The doctor adjusted his white shirt a little bit. "We can't just undo everything." The nurse looked at her feet, sniffling. He started clicking his pen nervously. "I'm sorry. You are going to have to learn to re-walk without them. There are a few things we can do, in your shoes and such, to make you as comfortable as possible, but it's difficult process to learn to walk when you have no toes."

Edward was not looking at either of them. His eyes were focused on the curtain. Standard hospital room curtain, hideous mint green color. Was it six feet tall or eight feet? He couldn't look at them.

"I'm so sorry," the nurse said, sniffling harder and suddenly exiting the room.

"Look, the rest of it..." The doctor sat on the edge of the bed. "Listen, we can fix eighty percent. Well, at least fifty percent of it. You won't ever be the same. But you won't have to keep this."

Edward clenched his jaw, trembling with rage. "Fifty percent? Fucking fifty percent is the best you can do?"

"It's not that easy. I mean, look at yourself. Have you even looked? Have you? This isn't something I can just snap my fingers and fix." The doctor was starting to shout. "I'm not a miracle worker! I didn't do this to you. I'm just trying to give you some semblance of a life."

"I thought tattoos could be removed now," Edward said. His words were limp, defeated.

"We sort of can; it'll take a while. Yes, we can make them look better. If tattoos were the only problem, it would be a lot easier to promise it. But the *burns*, goddamn it. Not only are they infected, but they have been tattooed over. Any improvement is just going to be a miracle."

Edward said nothing, staring at the hideous mint-colored curtain. He wondered idly if any of the staff ever stole them to use as massive shower curtains. If he wrapped them around his body, how many layers would it be when he got to the end? He'd be a human burrito. He grew numb.

"I am sorry." The doctor stood up, grasping

his clipboard. "I wish there was more I could do." He walked to the door and then paused. "Do you want me to call anyone?"

Edward turned his mutilated face back to the doctor and, with intensity, said, "Yes. Call her."

Jaspierre's Last Chance

CHAPTER

THIRTY-NINE

Chance was really tired, really fucking tired of waiting around.

All he needed was Edward to give Jaspierre the message. And then he'd just strut himself up to the front door like he belonged, and she would open it and welcome him.

It was strange that after her eager offer of oral bliss, she would just disappear. *Really fucking strange.* Okay, if he was honest with himself, it wasn't that strange. He expected so much more from Jaspierre than from a normal woman. Face it, she was no more special than any of the other slutty whores he slept with. She was just a bunch of warm holes too. He got all caught up with her letting him put it in and he completely lost sight of everything.

Why the hell was he building her a house,

preparing for their children, doing all this fucking shit, when she wasn't waiting for him? She wasn't doing anything, anything at all. She wasn't ready for him. She wouldn't even blow him on the side of the road. It was like she didn't like him. After he kept Lucille safe all these years? *What the hell did he have to do to impress her!*

Fuck. His legs still hurt where the bullet had punched through his meaty thigh. It still hurt a lot; in fact, it had grown red and infected. When he stared at it, he couldn't remember what happened.

Jaspierre, love of his life, left him to die. Again. Over and over, she would leave him to die. What the fuck was wrong with her?

He sat in his newly stolen blood red truck, right outside Jaspierre's perfect gate. He started to think that he could smell her, that her scent was drifting through the air erotically in front of him. The scent felt thick and tangible, like pudding. Like a thick vanilla pudding. He could feel the texture of it in his mouth, rolling across his tongue. He could taste her. She tasted like an adventure. She tasted like perfection baked with a little bit of hell.

He closed his eyes, remembering when he grew bigger and bigger and he almost exploded off the planet and somehow, somehow, she could still ground him. She pulled him out of space and time itself. She was the only woman who had ever done that. *The only woman who could do that.* All other women were inferior; that was why they were so weak. Women were weak, useless creatures. Men weren't any better. The only person on this entire planet who understood when he was starting to spiral out of control, and still managed to ground him, and still somehow managed to love him was Jaspierre.

Jaspierre was the only one who hadn't died. He would've killed her by now if she had stopped escaping. She was literally the only woman who hurt him. Physically injured him. How could she even do that? *He was invincible!* He could climb up a mountain after being smashed by a vehicle, completely uninjured. And yet somehow, she had burned him alive. Somehow, she had driven a knife into the crook of his neck, rendering him leaking blood for days on end. How could she do that? Was she kryptonite? She was his only weakness, his better half, and he was tired of waiting.

He slid big fat sunglasses over his scarred face. Then, he pressed the accelerator, revving the engine of the big truck he had stolen. He would be back in the morning and they would have it out. She owed him. He shifted the machine guns on the seat next to him.

Or she would give him back Lucille.

CHAPTER

FORTY

The Asian man was barely crisped in the fire when Jaspierre got a call.

Viscardine, her mother's website, had gone down. Jaspierre tried to register what this meant, but she couldn't process it. It had gone down, all the way down. More than half her staff had been arrested. All the secrets that Mother had for so long were suddenly revealed. In fact, the website itself had gone nuclear.

Dru had managed a final blow. The website somehow leaked information: addresses, phone numbers, names, and most importantly, crimes. Lots and lots and lots of criminal activity was revealed. Kyller and Co. would struggle in the wake. As far as Jaspierre knew, all of them had been hired from Viscardine. *Every single staff member.*

And at least half had already been arrested. If they were in prison, they wouldn't be back to work. Her cash-generating company had been decapitated at the head. She had no idea where she would hire more staff, or *how* to hire more staff. She didn't know how much Severina had set up that was illegal, but when the entire staff was made up criminal delinquents, it was very likely that the company did illegal things. It wasn't usually a big deal-- a community of criminals protects itself.

It was only a big deal if the community collapsed. She scrambled to see if she had any money left. If the coffers had been filled, even a little, before the crisis.

And yes, she had much more than she had had a week ago. About two million now. But it wasn't enough. She wasn't sure that she could single-handedly lift the company back to it glorious greatness. How could she do that with no capital?

Fucking Dru. He somehow had managed to destroy her. He was pretty damn invested in making her hurt. In making her writhe.

No. It wasn't *her*. He didn't want to hurt her. He wanted to hurt Severina. She was the woman he wanted to take down. She was dead. The best he could do was destroy her legacy, her daughter, her home.

And he was doing one hell of a job. Had done. He had done one hell of a job.

What the fuck was she supposed to do now? Work at McDonald's? It was laughable. Her empire would never be the same, not after this. She scheduled a board meeting, and an hour later, she was sitting at the head of table.

She waited, but it was futile. Not one board member showed. *Fuck, I am so screwed.* Fact was, she was still on probation. And even though she had quite comfortably skittered off to Canada and back, she couldn't possibly escape at least a slap on the wrist for fraternizing with criminals.

Her criminals--her staff. All of the cogs of her machine had fallen out. Did she know how to build it back together?

She had a daughter to think about, so she sure as hell was going to try.

JASPIERRE'S LAST CHANCE

CHAPTER

FORTY-ONE

Jaspierre, Arnold, and Lucille went down the stairs behind the fireplace. "I'm so sorry, I didn't really mean for it to go like this. I messed up," Arnold said quickly.

Jaspierre could immediately see the problem. The large, very angry Asian man wandering down the hallway at the bottom of the spiral staircase. He was mad as hell, slamming into the walls and repeatedly screaming at the top of his lungs. The room to his door was open.

"You let him out of his room," said Jaspierre.

"I didn't mean to. I'm sorry," Arnold said.

Jaspierre slipped in front of the controls, quickly switching levers, pressing buttons. A loud hissing noise started to curl from the downstairs hallway, but the Asian man did not fall unconscious.

"Shit. Dru must have used up all the gas," Jaspierre grabbed a lever, slid it out of the console, suddenly revealing a large, sharp blade. "At least he left this here. I'll have to take care of him the old-fashioned way – chop chop, here we go." She pressed one more button as she stood and walked to the door. The door, smooth and white at the top of the spiral staircase, slid open. The large Asian man charged up the spiral staircase; he was like a bear, a giant raving mad animal. His assault was so fast and so quick charging forward, that he knocked Jaspierre off her feet. Her blade was lodged deep in his belly, and she twisted it quickly. The man let out a cry of pain, and then immediately started convulsing, spurting blood all over her.

"Dammit. So fucking disgusting." Jaspierre wiggled and squirmed her way out from under the large, overweight man. "You have to clean this all up, Arnold. Fuck. That was not how I wanted this to go down."

Lucille suddenly let out a scream. Her hands covered her face, and she was terrified.

Jaspierre let out an exasperated scream of her own. "Lucille, calm down." The blood was still dripping off her dress, dripping off her blade. What was wrong with Lucille that she couldn't

understand that the world was kill or get killed?
"Lucille. He would have killed you. He would've
killed me, Arnold, and you. He would've killed
Tessa, Ikali, and those other little servals that you
haven't named yet. He is a mad man. So calm
down." She picked up Lucille and hugged her
tightly. "I'm sorry you got frightened." She
struggled to give her a choice. "Do you want to go
upstairs now or stay with me?" Lucille grabbed
her tightly.

Arnold was already grabbing his arm and
trying to drag the man upstairs. "Let's get him in
the fireplace. I'd like to get mopping." He didn't
say anything else, but Jaspierre could see his
mouth clicking the one-two-three-four over and
over and over. All this blood on these white floors
must have been driving him mad.

"Honey, I have to help get him upstairs
okay?" She kissed the little girl and set her back on
the floor. She grabbed the other arm and they
clunked the big massive man up the stairs while
Lucille stood trembling nearby. Once they loaded
him into the fireplace, Arnold disappeared back
down the stairs and Lucille and Jaspierre were left
in her office.

"Have you burned a corpse before?"
Jaspierre said to Lucille.

The little wide-eyed frightened girl shook

her head back and forth.

"I'm going to show you the woodpile. I would like you to bring wood in here, okay? I will take a shower and be right back." Jaspierre grabbed Lucille's little hand and took her outdoors to the woodpile. Without saying another word, she handed Lucille the handle to a small wooden wagon.

Jaspierre found herself racing up the stairs, showering quickly, her blood-soaked dress on the floor. She slipped on her grey soft T-shirt dress and raced back downstairs with a towel still on her head. She had forgotten to give Lucille a choice. Was she being a better mother yet? The child had seemed a lot calmer. Jaspierre felt different too, more concerned for her desires and less focused on making her talk.

"Have you ever even lit a fire before?" she said to the little girl, who was carefully pulling in her third wagon of wood. The pile wasn't very big yet. But she was studious and had not paused for even a moment the whole time Jaspierre was gone. Her bright blue eyes stared up at Jaspierre, and she shook her curls back and forth. *No.*

"Did you learn anything with those people? I bet they just gave you lollipops and told you to be a princess." Jaspierre grinned at her and then handed Lucille the little book of matches. She took her own book of matches and showed Lucille how to pull the match quickly to light it.

Lucille ruined five of ten matches before she finally got one to spark and light. When she finally got it, Lucille and Jaspierre smiled at each other. The beautiful bonding moment. A moment she remembered having with her mother, only with less hitting.

This wasn't like that; this was beautiful. The match went out long before Lucille could get a little piece paper lit that Jaspierre had sat on the bloody belly of the Asian man. But she had four more matches. By the time she finally got it lit, there were two matches left. Pretty damn good for a four-year-old.

"Good job." Jaspierre tried to remember any of the other details of the parenting book she had read. "You are very smart." Lucille looked up with big eyes and almost smiled.

They set all of the burned matches onto the piece of paper, building a little tiny bonfire.

She added a little bit of kindling, a few logs, and soon, maybe an hour into their little fire-building adventure, they had a real roaring bonfire. The kind worth jumping over.

Jaspierre looked at the little girl, and finally seemed to be smiling. "You did a really good job."

JASPIERRE'S LAST CHANCE

CHAPTER

FORTY-TWO

In the middle of the night, Jaspierre awoke with Ikali and Tessa curled on her bed. They hadn't slept in the same bed since before she had gone to prison. It was wonderful to have her moment. The world was almost right again.

But Kyller and Co. was on her mind, and despite her lovely pets giving her attention that she adored, she knew she had a people crisis. She couldn't hire any more of *the right kind of people.* That was what Mother called them. *The right kind of people.* Dru had called them that too.

She sat up straight when she suddenly realized what she did have. She had *people.* She had people in her basement. They might or might not suit her purposes, but they were certainly an excellent place to start. She rolled it around in her head. There were two beautiful ways to repurpose these people. The ones that weren't a good fit to work with--she could get them lumped in with the people being arrested; hell, maybe she could keep her best staff and simply rename them. It was an interesting idea, to place the malformed monsters in prison, and allow her staff to reign supreme.

She had finally started to learn how to be a good mama, and had solved part of the problem of the people in the basement. Now she still had to come up with a plan for Chance, for he would rear his ugly head any moment now.

She rested her hand on Tessa's sweet head, and they slept, sound and safe, together as family.

Chapter

Forty-Three

Jaspierre lifted Lucille into her car seat. The pride of being a proper mother was swelling in her chest. Lucille still hadn't spoken a word, but this whole give her two choices thing was working out great. "Do you want to go to get ice cream or a toy?" Jaspierre would hold out each hand like an option, and Lucille would point.

Then they'd both laugh and laugh and be happy forever. Lucille was so smart she helped Jaspierre buckle the seat, and then they rambled down the road together. They got ice cream at a little shop and Lucille sat across from Jaspierre and everything seemed wonderful. "So, Lucille, I came up with a great way to save the family business. And I'm so happy! You and I are good friends now, aren't we?"

Jaspierre's Last Chance

Lucille took a big bite of sprinkle-coated vanilla ice cream and gave a thumbs-up with her mouth full.

"I know we have had rather a rough start to things, but I think once Kyller and Co. gets back on track, we'll be doing great. Did you name any of the servals yet?"

Lucille made a thumbs-up again and continued eating her ice cream.

"I wish you'd just tell me! Do you want me to guess?" Jaspierre said, and they were both smiles and giggles. Sure, Lucille wasn't talking, but that raging anger that Jaspierre had been struggling with seemed to have dissipated. She had so much more compassion for the child and her struggles. It had been a hard week for the girl. This was the only time she really seemed to be happy. Jaspierre had been reading that children needed happy touches multiple times a day. She leaned forward and touched her arm gently.

"Are any of them named ice cream?"

Blond curls shook.

"Sprinkles?"

Lucille let out a snort, and almost choked on her ice cream. But before they could continue their little game, the phone rang. "Hello, this is Jaspierre."

"Ma'am, I'm a doctor down at St. Mary's

and I've got a Detective Edward Darbonne here,
and he's been asking for you. He's been in..."
There was a long pause. "...an accident. He could
really use a friend."

"I'm on my way." Jaspierre stood up,
clicking her phone off, nerves strung thin. "Lucille,
honey, I'm sorry. We were having so much fun,
but we have to go to the hospital. Edward has
been in an accident." She rolled the word around
in her mouth. The doctor had hesitated far too
long and an ominous feeling was creeping up
Jaspierre's back. She considered dropping Lucille
off at the house with Arnold, but that would be
almost two hours of driving the wrong direction.
She'd just have to tag along.

Jaspierre gripped Lucille's hand tightly as
they entered the hospital. "I'm here to see Edward
Darbonne?" The secretary recited his room
number with a pained look on her face.

"We're all so very sorry," she said, pressing
her hand softly into Jaspierre's.

Jaspierre's stomach flipped and she held
Lucille's hand tightly as they walked to the
elevator. Once inside, she pressed the third floor.
Her chest grew tight, and she looked down at the
little girl who was depending on her.

* * * * * * * * * * * *

Chance watched the two eating ice cream.

Jaspierre's Last Chance

He sat in the stolen red truck and watched with his binoculars. He had his machine gun warm on his lap. His whole body trembled with excitement. She answered the phone, and then they both stood up to leave. Once they were in her car, he followed along behind slowly. They went to the hospital.

Good. It was well beyond time for them to go to the hospital. Get a little message he left her. But as he impatiently waited in his truck, it seemed like it was taking too long. Had they left through a back door? What was going on? He stared at the entrance doors sliding open and shut as a group of people passed through. Fuck it. He couldn't wait any longer.

He stepped out of his car and took the machine gun with his twenty-five clips of ammo strapped to his chest.

Maybe he wanted to deliver this message himself.

CHAPTER

FORTY-FOUR

Jaspierre stood in the hallway of the hospital. Lucille held her hand tightly. Edward's doctor had called her and asked her to come talk to him.

Why hadn't Edward called her directly?

The hallway seemed too quiet, and she felt uneasy walking up to his room. She didn't know anything more, just that he had been hospitalized.

The sinking pit in her stomach was enough for her to know. Chance had done whatever she was about to see.

How had Edward survived it? Chance didn't seem to let many people live.

Lucille held her little hand. It would hopefully do Edward some good to see how the child was faring.

Finally, she opened the door.

"Edward?" she whispered tentatively. He seemed to be asleep. His face had been shredded and long black tattoo lines drawn across it. Both his feet were bandaged and lifted in a sling. His left arm was in a cast.

She recognized immediately what this meant. His toes had been removed. His arm would be broken; probably, he had been raped. This was Chance's signature, *his love note to her*. She stared, rage brewing inside her soul. An old hatred rekindled and ablaze; her whole world spun. And that was before he spoke.

"You left me." His tone was dead. He wouldn't turn his face any more towards her, not even flickering his eyes in her direction.

"When?"

"I ran across this country for you, I chased you to the ends of the earth, and you left me with him. *You left me for him to destroy*." His voice seemed raspy and painful.

It struck her suddenly what he meant. He meant Canada and only now did she realize that he was the one in the silver car. "I didn't know. I'm sorry." Her voice took a cold bite from the anger. From the rage. She should have killed Chance earlier. If he could even be killed.

He let out a hoarse cracking noise that sounded like the hint of a sob. She couldn't give him anything more. Her heart had frozen over, and every ounce of his pain was absorbed into the black hole of her heart.

He coughed, holding back his tears. "He gave me a message."

Her eyes grew wide.

"You fucking owe him."

Jaspierre's Last Chance

Chapter

Forty-Five

Jaspierre stepped into the elevator to leave the hospital more ready than she had ever been. This was what she had trained for.

When she was in prison, assuming Lucille dead, she had trained and prepped and planned for one thing, and one thing only.

And now it was time. Her heart was pounding feverishly inside her. Lucille's tiny hand held hers. She couldn't stop the grin from creeping across her lips as she pressed the button for the ground floor. She'd go home and get her blade, she had a small one strapped to her leg like always, but she wanted the big one. The doors opened at the bottom and there he was.

"*Mine Forever*" sparkled on her neckline.

She nodded before he spoke, already agreeing.

"You owe me." Chance wasn't even trying to hide himself, his scarred, tattooed flesh revealed for the world to see. No hat. No sunglasses. He had his gun out, a machine gun of some sort, if Jaspierre could recognize such things. He pressed the tip of the gun against the elevator door, holding it open. Jaspierre scanned the room, more out of habit than any need to know.

Bodies lay crumpled everywhere. The wall had a little dotted line of bullet holes. Here and now, this was where it would end. Lucille quivered behind her mother.

"Give her back or pay me what I am owed." The large gun swung its nose to the little girl's blond curls. Her beautiful blue eyes grew wide with fright.

"Lucille." Jaspierre's voice was cold and distant. She pointed to the desk and Lucille nodded and started to run. Chance swung the tip of the gun to follow the small child as she scrambled. But Jaspierre was already upon him. Her body tumbled against his and they were down. Her breasts were pressed tightly against his skin, and his erection was already throbbing for more.

"Mine Forever" dangled in front of his nose.

"You owe me!" he screamed, bellowing his horny hateful noise into her neck, kissing at her in a frantic way.

She smiled, a hot, sexy smile of a girl who has just been told she is beautiful. A girl who just finally believed it. His gnarled lips attacked her neck and his dick was firm between her thighs. She let out a soft gasp and pressed her nose against his.

His eyes grew soft staring at hers. And they froze like that, breathless and wonderful right before she pulled out the blade. She drove it downward and he bucked up with his hips, blocking her with the machine gun. She wobbled, and he let out a hot and dirty cry of pleasure.

"Fuck, Jaspierre, fuck, don't. *Fuck*." He had a desperate ring to his voice.

JASPIERRE'S LAST CHANCE

CHAPTER

FORTY-SIX

Her breasts were so close to his face he could taste them. Saliva dripped from his mouth. He had to have her. She could fucking shoot him, stab him, rip off his arms, as long as his cock got to nestle in her fuckhole. *No, her pussy.* Her fucking pussy.

He roared to life again as she desperately swung her little knife. He had never been so alive. He was more alive than anyone had ever been in the entire universe. His cock held half his blood and still he had room to think, to block with his gun. His arms knew no limits, and he rolled her underneath him, she kept futilely pressing the blade tight against the machine gun. Tossing her underneath him made the gun slip slightly, and the blade pierced his chest at least an inch. *Fuck, it was good.*

Jaspierre's Last Chance

He shoved both her hands above her head, holding them down with the gun.

And they kissed. She kissed him just as hard as ever. Just as fucking delicious as the very first time.

"I love you, Jaspierre." His hoarse, growling voice said the words he had never before uttered aloud as a man.

She gasped, a hot, breathless cry of pleasure. *She loved him!*

He started grinding against her and said another word he had never bothered with before. "Please?" He let a soft little whimper trickle off his tongue as his eager cock throbbed against her moist place.

She let out the prettiest smile he had ever seen. *Jaspierre.* His beautiful soon-to-be bride. The only woman he had ever loved. *Fuck, the only person who had ever loved him.*

His mind raced back to the first moment she had loved him. They had been so little. Mere children. And she had helped him burn his first corpse.

22 Years Earlier

Jaspierre cocked her head to the side curiously. She hadn't said anything yet, and Chance wasn't sure she would.

"Are you mad at me?" Finally, he said, slowly, unable to look at her little brown nine-year-old eyes any longer. Chance was only ten himself. Jaspierre hadn't reacted as strongly as he had expected.

"Why would I be mad at you?" she asked, wrinkling her brow.

"Did you kill your Mother?" he said again. He hadn't seen Severina in at least a year, maybe even longer.

"She is just on a business trip. I've said that." Jaspierre lied again, but she kept staring with those big eyes. It was as if she was searching inside his soul.

"I was kind of hoping you had..." He paused and bit his lip nervously. "If you did kill her, what would you do with her body?"

She sat down on the steps and let out a long breath. "I'd burn if, of course. Don't you know anything? Didn't Liddy teach you how to do that? Sometimes I wonder if she's taught you a damn thing." Jaspierre wasn't one to curse but sometimes, she let it slip out. It felt especially grown up.

"I didn't kill her. I don't know where she is. She just... vanished." Jaspierre didn't say Mother went missing when she let out Pierre and Jasper. That somehow, moments before, that was the last time she had seen her mother.

She wished she knew where Severina was. She wished it so hard it made her stomach hurt. Jaspierre tried not to think of it; she hated to cry in front of Chance. He always took it so personally.

"Jaspierre." He snapped her attention back to her. He was in front of her, his big beautiful eyes staring into hers. "How hard is it to burn a body?"

Jaspierre let out a long sigh. "Who did you kill?" That was it. No judgment, no surprise. He was going to marry this girl someday. She could take such an enormous secret in one breath without even the slightest hint of worry. He would have kissed her right then and there if he thought he knew how to do it.

"I-I don't think you want to know."

She stood up suddenly and clapped her hands together, dusting them off. "We're gonna have to drag it to the office. You might as well let me know. Where did you put her?" Jaspierre continued; she had a little edge to her voice now. A hint of coldness. That coldness had a tremble to it, and he could see her eyes grow shinier and shinier like magic. They grew so shiny and bright he could see his own face reflected in them, and as he stared, his heart thumping, he saw his reflection step out of her eye and run down her cheek. She was crying.

"Don't cry, Jasp. You don't have to help."

"She's my mother. I'm the only one who has to be there." Her tiny voice was calm, but her body shuddered as the words slipped through her lips.

"Your...? Wait, no, Jasp." The little girl didn't turn her head, using every muscle in her body to control the terrified sobs. "No! Jaspierre! It's not your mother. I didn't kill her. Believe me! I would have if I thought it would have helped you, but I didn't kill her!" Chance grabbed the little girl and kissed her forehead in a sweet gesture. His voice cracked as he continued. "I didn't kill *your* mother." He emphasized the word tightly, and his stomach flipped as he told her his biggest secret ever. "It was Liddy. I killed *my* Liddy. I shouldn't have done it. I shouldn't have. She just made me so mad, and she just stood there and let everything happen." He was suddenly racked with his own sobs, burying his head into her tiny shoulder. "I'm so sorry, Jaspierre. Please forgive me. I know you loved her."

And then, in the best moment of his entire life, she said, "You really would have killed Mother for me?"

"Yes, Jaspierre. I'd do anything for you."

"I love you," she whispered into his stringy brown hair, her tiny voice mending his heart and breaking it all over again. She wrapped herself around him perfectly, sweet and innocent with no understanding of the way his heart was pounding inside him. He kissed her softly, on the lips, the way a man did to a woman in the movies. And both of them, tear-stained and giggling, went skipping away to the corpse.

It was the first day that he believed she loved him back. The first day that he had been swallowed alive by her love. He would never forget it. He would never let her go. She was forever his.

CHAPTER

FORTY-SEVEN

Jaspierre writhed below Chance, screaming and pushing him away while he kissed at her frantically. He was gone. It was like he wasn't in the room anymore. She knew it, but did he? She stopped struggling, and he just continued kissing her and saying over and over that he loved her.

She found her heart pounding, and her grin became uncontrollable. A laugh was bubbling up her throat and out her lungs before she could check it. *He was insane!* It struck her as so funny that she let out another hysterical laugh, almost dropping her knife as she cackled.

She took a deep breath and looked at the man still kissing down her neck, her hands still pressed tightly to the floor with the machine gun. "It's been so long, Chance, I'm not even sure we know how to do this anymore."

He looked at her with his dark eyes and they focused on her, and then went wild again. He was gone. Whatever it was he was experiencing wasn't in this room anymore. She smiled and adjusted her hips underneath him. She scanned the room; there was a dead woman lying not two feet away. She had dark hair and large breasts. Would Chance realize she was slipping him farther and farther onto a dead woman? Quickly, she shifted, scooting closer to the woman. She somehow thought that maybe he wouldn't even notice. He'd just fuck himself exhausted before he finally realized he was plowing his seed into the dead instead of her.

He might even like it more.

Jaspierre stared at him while he kept humping at her, holding her wrists with the gun. "Chance?" she said, and he let out a moan of delight. She tried to shift herself closer to the corpse.

"Say it again, baby."

He couldn't get his pants off with his hands pressed into the gun, holding her hands steady. He was already starting to shift so he could free one hand to let loose the kraken. Jaspierre glanced up at his hands, planning the exact moment to throw her weight and stab him again. But with a gasp, she realized the machine gun was pointed at the desk. Those frightened blue eyes peeked out from the desk, and Chance shoved his weight into the gun, shifting himself to try to free his hand. Jaspierre let out a scream as the gun suddenly fired.

It woke him. He was back, his eyes clear as day, mad as fucking hell. "I would have killed her for you if I thought it would have helped."

"She was my mother. I should have killed her myself," Jaspierre replied, her head spinning from the rickety *pop pop pop* of the bullets. Lucille was silent. *Surely even a mute would scream if you shot them.*

Surely she would scream.

Scream.

Please.

Hot tears started to surge and Jaspierre fought to hold them down.

Fucking scream already.

Chance threw his body against her, knocking her breathless, and he struggled to unbutton with one hand. But it was enough; her right hand freed momentarily as he jerked his cock out. The blade slid into his buttocks, the only place she could reach to jab, and his cock jumped, thrusting harder from the pain. "Fuck, get your fucking panties off!" He tore at them frantically, finally able to slide past them into her. He wasn't even trying to stop her, just desperately needing to fuck. She let out a scream of pain and pleasure and the knife kept stabbing, digging into him over and over, into his ass, his thigh, his back, his side.

Fucking and dying.

"Jaspierre, you are going to kill me. Just let me finish, dammit!" he screamed into her face, fucking hard and fast, screaming at every slip of the blade. "You owe me!" It pierced him, and he pierced into her, thrashing, blood and sex and sweat soaking them both. She drove it in again, without hesitation. He screamed again, fucking harder. She stabbed him fifteen times before he came, pulsing deep into her.

He wept, kissed her, and told her he loved her. "You have always been mine forever. I've never felt more loved than now," he whispered, spent, and collapsed on her, gushing and bleeding.

She writhed underneath him. Her blade pierced him, twisting five more times. "You were my best friend. I loved you too," she said. Halfheartedly, she kept swinging and stabbed him five more times before he finally shuddered and died. The sobs bucked out of her. He was her only true friend. "Why did you make me kill you?"

She wept and held him as he grew cold in

her arms. When her world finally stopped spinning, she slowly rolled him off of her and left the knife, still twisted in his cold back. "I don't have anything else to live for," she whispered. Sirens were starting to wail in the distance. She should just let them come.

She sat up slowly, blood-soaked and broken.

Her sobs grew as cold as he had, her empty heart hardening again, and then she heard it. They weren't just her sobs. She flickered her eyes up to the sound, and Lucille stood in front of her with big sobbing eyes.

"Lucille! I thought you were dead. I thought..." Jaspierre reached for the little girl, both blood-soaked hands outstretched.

"You killed my dad," Lucille said, sobbing little tiny choking noises. "You killed my dad!" Suddenly, the little girl screamed it. "You killed him dead. You killed him dead!" Her voice was cracking with terror.

"I'm sorry." Jaspierre scooped up the child and held her tight. "I had to. I'm so sorry; he was a bad man."

"I didn't think anyone could kill him," Lucille said, and hugged her mama tightly. "Can we go home now?"

Jaspierre knew for the very first time that

Jaspierre's Last Chance

they were all going to be okay.

JASPIERRE
JASPIERRE'S DESCENT
JASPIERRE'S LAST CHANCE
SEVERINA-
JASPIERRE BEGINS

LANDLOCKED LIGHTHOUSE
PADLOCKED PENTHOUSE

WWW.MIXIJAPPLEBOTTOM.COM

A Note from Mixi...

Thank you for reading Jaspierre's Last Chance. *I'd really appreciate a review if you aren't too busy!*

Ready for the sequel? **Severina-Jaspierre Begins-** Here you will get to find out who killed Severina!

Here is a little excerpt:

Severina nodded her head slowly. She was a really lucky kid to have this house and these parents. And an uncle. A brand new uncle who was a little messed up. She couldn't wait to meet him. She was nine and plenty old enough to learn about her family, and her home. She stood up slowly, adjusting her skirt. It was one of her favorite skirts, and she was really disappointed that it had gotten stained. She brushed at it with her hand slowly.

It was a big splotch right near the hem. Maybe it wouldn't be so noticeable if she spun. She twirled quickly, but it was still really easy to see. She sat back down, frowning at it, rubbing her right hand on it a little harder. Maybe if she licked it off?

Jaspierre's Last Chance

She lifted the hem towards her mouth and the cop sitting near her suddenly looked up at her. She paused, the skirt nearly at her lips. "Oh geez. Let's go get you something clean to wear." The cop was a girl cop, she had her hair in a bun underneath her little black cap. Her shiny badge flickered, and she yanked the dress out of Severina's hand. She lifted the child up, and they walked into the large door. Inside was an ancient marble floor in desperate need of refinishing. The cop shielded Severina's eyes as they tromped upstairs quickly.

In the center of the room there were more cops all standing hushed around mommy and daddy. Severina tried to peer around the edge of the cop, but she quickly blocked her. "Don't look, we just have to get you something to wear."

Severina's room was the first door on the right, and they slipped inside quickly and quietly. The cop rummaged through her closet and handed her a simple pair of pants and a shirt. Severina frowned. "I pick my own clothes. I'm not going to wear that. There are a lot of camera's here."

Severina stepped to the closet and pulled out a long dress dotted with sequins at the collar. The cop frowned. "You..." The cop paused. The kid just lost both parents. If she wanted to be overdressed, so be it. "Alright."

As Severina changed she put the stained skirt on the bed. The cop was gathering some things, a nightgown and some sensible clothing, and while she wasn't looking Severina quickly licked the stain.

It didn't taste like blood any more.

I am currently living in a five story house I am remodeling. I'm almost done with the fourth and fifth floors and man, am I tired. More books to come. If you want to hear when my next book is out, sign up for my newsletter.

Thanks so much!

Mixi J Applebottom

Feel free to contact Mixi directly at:
mixijapplebottom@gmail.com

Join my email list:
mixijapplebottom.com/mailing-list